DATE DUE

MY 13 '94			
DE 23 '94			
JY 8 '97			
OC 10 '00			
AP 25 '01			
MY 14 '01			
AG 5 '04			

of ITALY

Sicily, Sardinia, and the Aeolian Islands

Ticknor & Fields
New York
1991

BARBARA GRIZZUTI HARRISON

PHOTOS BY SHEILA NARDULLI

For information about permission to
reproduce selections from this book, write
to Permissions, Ticknor & Fields,
Houghton Mifflin Company, 2 Park Street,
Boston, Massachusetts 02108

Library of Congress
Cataloging-in-Publication Data

Harrison, Barbara Grizzuti.
The islands of Italy : Sicily, Sardinia,
and the Aeolian Islands / Barbara Grizzuti
Harrison ; with photos by Sheila Nardulli.
     p.   cm.
ISBN 0-395-59302-6
1. Sicily (Italy) — Description and travel
— 1981–   2. Sardinia (Italy) —
Description and travel — 1981–
3. Lipari Islands — Description and
travel.   4. Harrison, Barbara Grizzuti —
Journeys — Italy.   5. Authors,
American — 20th century — Journeys —
Italy.   I. Nardulli, Sheila.   II. Title.
DG864.2.H37   1991   91-2887
914.5′804928 — dc20   CIP

Printed in Hong Kong

FCI 10 9 8 7 6 5 4 3 2 1

Design by Karen Salsgiver

Contents

A well,
Panarea.

Introduction

It is tempting to say that one visits the islands of Italy simply because they are beautiful and because they are there, which would of course be reason enough — except that no act has a single motive.

I went because of my love of water, which is mingled with and almost indistinguishable from a fear of water (I can float in a vertical position — I enter a fugue state — but I cannot bear to bury my face in water).

I went as a kind of memorial gift to my father, who, though he lived ten miles from the sea in Calabria, never saw the sea until he crossed it to come to America (over sixty years later, when he was dying, he made another crossing, almost as terrible as that first one: he crossed the bridge from Brooklyn to Manhattan to visit Mott Street and Hester Street and Mulberry Street, where he had grown up, but to which, in adulthood, for dark reasons that I can sometimes intuit — reasons having to do with love and betrayal and loss — he had never once returned).

I went, as a supplicant, to search once again for my mother and ask forgiveness of her spirit . . . which is to say, to try once again to comprehend the mystery of her life: water was one of the pleasures she banished, as she banished all earthly pleasure with fierce will, from her days. (I have never known why she was so dedicated to pain.)

I went for my Grandma DiNardo, fat and rosy and jolly in her long black wool bathing suit with remarkable décolletage, who played Ring Around the Rosie with me — just with me — at Coney Island, the froth of waves licking at our ankles. I cherish this image of play, and my gratitude to her was a driving force, too.

I went because the islands of Italy combine all the elements — fire, water, earth, and air — and that is irresistible.

I went to look for a dusty square that exists in my imagination: paths from the green countryside converge on a buttery yellow church and in this crossroad stands perpetually a woman dressed in black, a donkey, baskets of flowers . . . I almost thought to find this square in Corleone, but I did not. What I found instead in Sicily surprised and confounded me.

I went because water reconciles me to the hard world of stone . . .

And because the islands are so beautifully there.

Barbara Grizzuti Harrison

Confess what you are smuggling: Moods, states of grace, elegies.

— Italo Calvino, *Invisible Cities*

The ISLANDS of ITALY

The fact is that a journey is like a representation of life, a synthesis of all its elements,

contracted in space and time; rather like a play, indeed; and it recreates, with a wealth

of hidden artifice, all those elements, those influences and relationships which

constitute our existence. — Leonardo Sciascia, *The Wine-Dark Sea*

This violence of landscape, this cruelty of climate, this continual tension in everything, and these monuments, even, of the past, magnificent yet incomprehensible because not built by us and yet standing around like lovely mute ghosts; all those rulers who landed by main force from every direction, who were at once obeyed, soon detested, and always misunderstood, their only expressions works of art we couldn't understand and taxes which we understood only too well and which they spent elsewhere: all these things have formed our character, which is thus conditioned by events outside our control as well as by a terrifying insularity of mind. — Giuseppe di Lampedusa, *The Leopard*

SICILY

Taormina,
the garden of the San Domenico hotel,
once a monastery.

"Bring me within your hands that flower which yearns
Up to the ultimate transparent white
Where all of life into its essence burns:
Bring me that flower impassioned of the light."
— Eugenio Montale, translated by Maurice English

Cities, like dreams, are made of desires and fears, even if the thread of their discourse is secret, their rules are absurd, their perspectives deceitful, and everything conceals something else. . . . You take delight not in a city's seven or seventy wonders, but in the answer it gives to a question of yours. — Italo Calvino, *Invisible Cities*

Etna.

Mountains, Mafia, marzipan. Solitary Greek temples, manic Spanish baroque, Moorish vermilion cupolas and golden Byzantine churches. Cloistered pleasure gardens, stern Norman forts. Market bazaars in which the North African and the Mediterranean, the savory and the seedy, mingle and mix: hot surprises in dark places. Seas of honey-colored wheat. Blood. Closed, secretive faces; chivalrous men; imperturbable courtesy. The world of the worldly rich and the world of the vanquished and lonely and poor. The elegant and the brutish.

The nourishing sea. The savage sun.

"The one place in Sicily I can *absolutely* recommend," says my fastidious friend Vittorio, concierge at the Albergo del Sole in Rome, "is Taormina"; he means the international sea resort is amazingly pretty. Also clean. And that it comes at one with few disagreeable or bewildering surprises, it is in no way shocking.

Taormina, flowery, refined, sophisticated, was favored by eighteenth-century travelers and loved by Garbo and by Goethe — who was enchanted by its roses and its nightingales and ravished by "the purity of the sky, the tang of the sea air, the haze which, as it were, dissolved mountains, sky and sea into one element" — and by Tennessee Williams and Truman Capote, who stayed at the San Domenico, a converted fifteenth-century monastery with sheltered cool cloisters rendered almost feverish by promiscuous purple bougainvillea, rooms richly furnished and still filled with the antiseptic light of celibacy.

Women with masses of expensive hair sit in the piazza and sip almond milk . . . and perhaps I am churlish, but it seems to me that what was once altogether sweet and wild — pink pensiones on black volcanic cliffs, the thrusting rocks and Homeric grottoes of the Ionian Sea — has been overly cultivated: not eradicated, but tamed. Before I saw Taormina, I would not have thought it possible to find a place beautiful and likable but not commensurately admirable.

There are in fact three Taorminas. There is the Taormina of the silky sea — the bathing lido and little fishing settlements and modern hotels filled with scoured air and almost clinical in their clean white severity. There is the little town, high up on a rocky balcony and reachable by cable car or motor car (for which, of course, this being Italy, there is no parking space; daily dramas have as their protagonists cars). And there is the still-wild mountain country above the charming town . . .

The long, determined Corso Umberto I, the main (and inescapable) street of Taormina, delivers you from one end of town to the other, its narrowness of purpose redeemed by piazzas and panoramic belvederes that rhythmically open the straight thoroughfare up when it threatens to become claustrophobic. Crooked little streets branch off from the Corso; arches frame the sea on one side, the hills — doves, cats, cattle — on the other. Antique jewelry and rare Sicilian amber are found in elegant shops with nineteenth-century storefronts, and tourist kitsch, too, and overpriced restaurants; never mind: balconies spill over with flowers to soften the austere fronts of ancient buildings, sculpted Roman medallions and Greek columns and capitals are built into buttery yellow facades. And there is marzipan (edible still lifes informed with a Renaissance love of color — some compensation, perhaps, for the Renaissance having

largely passed Sicily by); and there is black sugar candy made to look like lava, which parents — so indulgent are the Italians — give to naughty children.

The Corso empties into the Via del Teatro Greco, which climbs steeply to a much-admired Greco-Roman amphitheater. From the gladiatorial theater that once accommodated more than five thousand spectators, one can see the Aeolian Sea, Calabria, and Etna-mantled-in-snow. (Etna is seldom mentioned without its mantle of snow being mentioned; and it is *comme il faut* to find it beautiful, which is perhaps why Evelyn Waugh claimed to find it "repulsive.")

Mount Etna is always on the boil, fuming, its rivers of lava, for the time being, dammed. Video-cassettes of Etna in full eruptive fury, red hot lava cascading, are sold on the Corso, a form of superstition, a way of trivializing the catastrophic, taming the future, and making entertainment out of devastation; whistling past the graveyard and nostalgia for survived tragedy . . . all those things.

We went to pay our respects to Etna one sunny day — and found ourselves in an empty parking lot. "Etna is closed," said the attendant at the foot of that pagan mountain. "Closed?" "Closed till May 15," he said; and he thought our merry laughter was rude.

To get to Etna we had driven through blank stony towns where silent stone-faced men congregated; we passed butchers that sold *castrato* beef, and lemon trees and blossoming apple trees and houses made of lava with gardens in which long-stemmed artichokes like exotic flowers grew (and roses big as dinner plates). We visited a cemetery, too — a nicely domestic cemetery where Mary was enshrined behind glass and (as good housekeeping

"Homer, though he describes the most delicate food of the Greeks as made of flour, cheese, and honey, yet two of his similes are drawn from fishing. And Ulysses, when pretending to be poor and asking alms of one of the suitors, tells him that to hospitable kings, that is to those who are charitable to poor wanderers, the gods give seas abounding in fish, which are the greatest delight of the table."
— *Giambattista Vico*

and decorum require) window curtains framed the Queen of Heaven, who smiled as demurely as a new bride waiting for company in a polished kitchen. On one grave were the words (and these alone) MAMMA MAMMA. Rose bowers framed Etna in the near distance.

Then we climbed in the other direction to wild Mount Venero, taking our chances on roads that looped like ribbons of intestines, passed by hooting trucks carrying tons of oranges in nets that looked none too secure (their horns played the theme from *The Godfather*). "There would be something Zen about slipping on an orange peel and dying on a road lined with flowering chestnut trees and mimosa," someone said. ("No there wouldn't," said I.) Terraced folds of green velvet hills overlooking the sea. Wild flowering fennel, bitter yellow; wild garlic. Sea breeze and marguerites, blue fluorescent flowers of ice plant, and succulents. Olives, thistle, rock. Empty shells to mark the places hunters have been . . . We hear their bells before we see the goats and sheep. They blanket the road, they are like a swarm of bees in lapidary air . . . From mountains we see mountains; then we turn and see the sea and, far below, oily bodies on the beach. The wind howls and buffets our car. We are very high. Alone and high, built into a rock face, is a church: the Sanctuary of Santa Maria della Rocca, a church carved from a grotto, fitted into a cave. Outside, a rusty anchor recalls sailors dead at sea. The church, on this windswept cliff, is closed. I peer through a grille and see banks of red candles and mountain walls whitewashed and decorated: pink and blue and pretty, floral; just like Taormina. Someone has set out a meal in a red plastic bowl for a mangy orange cat.

PALERMO. On one side of the sea road from the airport to my hotel is the happy Mediterranean juxtaposition of date palms and pines, Christmas in July. Pink fleshy hibiscus and oleander which is deadly and prickly pears with elegant pale green flowers . . . what profligacy . . . But on the other side of the road are scrub and inhospitable hills — God is giving you a geography lesson: now you see me, now you don't; nature is profligate and varied, it is fickle too.

(So profligate that Goethe formed the fancy that he could discover here the "Primal Plant" — the plant from which all other plants were descended.)

Palermo is fabulous, intoxicating. And dangerous, too. Dangerous to the senses, upon which it places extravagant demands. And menacing — a city from which God often seems strangely absent: "God made the world," an unemployed Sicilian tells Danilo Dolci, "and put it into the hands of men. Can He always give His mind to what's going on there? . . . God's in the church and has His own affairs to attend to."

Palermitani say their city is "degradato" — degraded, afflicted with corruption and decay, vile poverty and ugly suburbs into the building of which washed Mafia money has gone. Their love is darkened — and deepened — by grief.

Who would guess that the tiny whiteness of jasmine could release such an abundance of sweet perfume?

Severity, excess, absurdity, grandeur: in the center of Palermo, Spanish baroque and Moorish and Byzantine and Norman dazzlingly coexist; whoever conquered — Berber emir, Byzantine, Spanish viceroy — left his mark in stone.

Frothy, grimy, restless, at the intersection of two main streets are the Quattro Canti (the four corners), actually a monument in four elliptical parts, orchestral, silly, eventually rather lovable, that marks the division of the city into four parts; one fits into the four corners as snugly as Palermo fits between the mountains and the sea. Seventeenth-century architects had the same horror of a vacuum that later Victorians did; the monument, which D. H. Lawrence called "that decorative maelstrom and [with reference to the chaotic traffic at the four corners] death trap," is alive with statues of rulers and patron saints . . . including poor Saint Agatha, who sliced her breasts off to make her less desirable to men, and offered them to God . . . Lampedusa writes of "virgin's cakes shaped like breasts . . . Saint Agatha's sliced-off breasts, made at convents, devoured at dances." In my memory (memory being a form of desire) the four canted monuments make a perfect circle climbing almost to the sky, enclosing me in this voluptuous city.

In nearby Piazza Bellini are three churches so different one from the other that they might have been built to honor and house several gods radically different in purpose and in temperament.

Goethe said that the churches of Palermo "surpass even those of the Jesuits in splendour, but accidentally, not deliberately. It's as if an artisan, a carver of figures or foliage, a gilder, a varnisher or a worker in marble, without taste and without guidance, had wished to show what he could do in a given spot."

As the Spaniards — dark, passionate, mystical — differed so much from the Romans — earthy, pragmatic, exuberant — so do the Spanish baroque churches of Palermo differ from the baroque churches of Rome. In the overbearing richness of

their decoration, in the redundancy of ornamentation, they are as irritable as the fires of the Inquisition (the Spanish brought as much energy to one as they did to the other); behind its sober doors, the church of Santa Caterina looks as if it will (like fire) of itself be consumed, as if it will fall of the weight of its own excrescences. The central dome of the nave, solidly encrusted, barnacled with meaningless gold, has spawned lesser domes in the transepts; saints dressed like cardinals frolic in skies of pale blue; lasciviously dimpled *putti* — marble cherubs indistinguishable from cupids — fly through pink sunsets trailing ribbons and garlands; marble — draped, folded, scalloped, serpentine — is heaped upon marble. Nothing is unelaborated upon; and the effect of all this is darkness and languor, not light.

In this perversely somber place a long-haired young girl wearing shorts makes her confession to a priest who inclines toward her sweetly in the open confessional (even the confessionals have domes), this transaction, anonymously public, is so friendly as to appear casual. A young man in dungarees and a checked red shirt reads the Liturgy of the Word, oblivious of gold . . .

FRUIT SELLER,
RAGUSA IBLA.

"In this secret island, where houses are barred and peasants refuse to admit they even know the way to their own village in clear view on a hillock within a few minutes' walk from here, in spite of the ostentatious show of mystery, reserve is a myth."
— *Lampedusa*, The Leopard

The lovely church of La Martorana has walls of gold, too, but its Byzantine mosaics tell rapturous stories with dignity; La Martorana is intimate and mysterious, it is gorgeous, it is an Arabian nights cave, a child's dream of a cave, a womb of light . . .

One day we saw a fat sweaty bride at La Martorana. In the piazza a baby had convulsions and fell out of its cradle, and the bride was protected from knowledge of this. Next to the bride's car is a car on which a scribbled sign is posted: SINCE MAY PEOPLE HAVE BEEN SLEEPING IN THIS CAR CERVICAL CANCER EMBOLISM. . . . There is a baptism in La Martorana, several baptisms in the Greek rite, chatty and ambulatory. Boys in bow ties and short black pants and girls in white hold candles against the gold: light unto light. Baby boys and baby girls spectacularly dressed are undressed and immersed in a copper vessel, then toweled off and clasped to their parents' proud breasts. Light heals, water heals. St. Paul says that in Christ there are no males and no females; in the first step of their spiritual journey, the babies are equal in the sight of God and congregants . . . It was in this church that marzipan was first made, and sold.

Rectangular, linear, strong, severely Moorish, the chapel of San Cataldo shares a mossy little courtyard — it always smells of country rain — with Martorana. Three melon-colored domes reach into an impeccably blue sky. Lampedusa compared these domes to flattened breasts, empty of milk . . .

One day at lunch in the trattoria in Piazza Bellini I ate half a roast chicken flavored with marjoram, and a chardlike vegetable served cold with olive oil and lemon, and cold white wine — the antithesis of the baroque. Another day I eat a pizza with smoked salmon and tomato and thyme; the salmon matches, in the dry transparency of the air, the domes of San Cataldo.

On the doors of San Cataldo and Santa Caterina there is a poster of a poised and pretty little girl, smiling: RAPITA, the poster says — KIDNAPED.

CASA PROFESSA,
PALERMO.

"It was the religious houses which gave the city its grimness and its character, its sedateness and also the sense of death which not even the vibrant Sicilian light could ever manage to disperse. . . . All Sicilian expression, even the most violent, is really wish-fulfillment: our sensuality is a hankering for death; our laziness, our spiced and drugged sherbets, a hankering for voluptuous immobility, that is, for death again; our meditative air is that of a void wanting to scrutinize the enigmas of nirvana."
— *Giuseppe di Lampedusa,* The Leopard

Under the stunning sun the huge market of La Vucciria is draped with awnings, faded green, blue, orange; under the swaybacked awnings naked electric light bulbs burn all day long. One is never quite in sunlight, never quite in shadow; this is a contained city, both homely and exotic, of booths and tents, a *souk*.

The stall keepers vie with one another for inventiveness and volume and ribaldry: *My lettuce is as sweet as milk. My pears are tender as butter. Your breasts are like two pomegranates, here are pomegranates hard and delicious as your breasts.* Meat looks still sensate, and sacrificial — whole lambs with imploring milky eyes and blood-wet hair, their bellies split open to expose the health of iridescent, obscenely pale pink internal organs, the gash held tidily together with bamboo skewers. The vulnerability of flesh. Sartre — the thought of whom, his forced rationality, his reflexive dread, is ludicrous in this candid oriental bazaar — said that to love a human being one had to imagine his intestines and love them too. Ropes of goats' intestines, small intestines snowy white, large intestines ivory, are wrapped around wooden skewers. They are quite pretty, as an abstraction, a kind of rubbery, slidy, slippery organic macrame. It doesn't do to entertain them in the imagination too long. Fish: pink; coral; silver; sluglike; squishy; hard; palpable; russet; pearly; mottled; striped; openmouthed in arrested wonder, and intelligent-looking. Snails

the size of thumbnails move in their baskets, a death dance. Livid *baccalà* surrounded by bright yellow tomatoes on improvised fountains made of pierced display tins — fountains among fountains in a city of extravagantly ugly fountains. Poor swordfish, futile great white eyes, futile, impotent beaks. *Hack!* goes the butcher, the fishmonger, on round sections of tree trunk supported on sturdy poles — no sanitized deception here. Smooth squashes, four feet long, of tender green culminating in decorative curlicues resting in nests of fuzzy green leaves. Four kinds and colors of eggplant. Music vaguely Arabian (perhaps this is my imagination) comes from the booths; and Madonna sings. A bakery with oven doors that resemble the façade of Santo Spirito in Florence: *panna brioche*, fat sandwiches filled with thick white cream.

In my immigrant family's southern Italian dialect, the word for squash, which I heard as *gugooz*, was used with a characteristic combination of affection and derision: Hey, *gugooz* . . . Hey, sweet nuisance, honeybunch-fool. Another word for squash, a word I heard as *zhoodrool*, signified only derision and contempt and was reserved for people outside the family. And the word for eggplant, which I heard as *mulinyam*, was applied to colored people. My family being Calabrese and Abruzzese, *Sicilians* were called *mulinyam*. They were thought, not without a shred of historical justification, to be Moors.

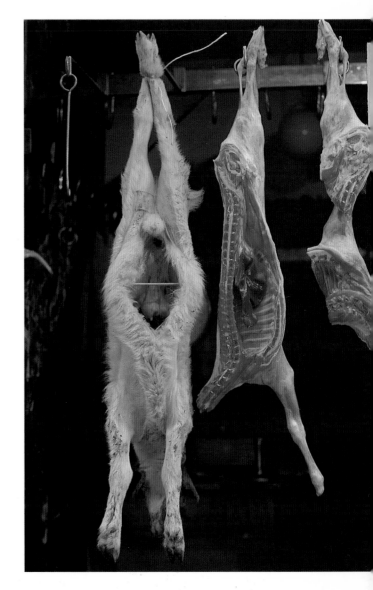

"A Jesuit priest, Father Kircher, once asserted that
on the coast of Sicily 'the shells of shell-fish, after
being ground to powder, come to life again and
start reproducing, if this powder is sprinkled with
salt water.' The Abbé de Vallemont cites this fable
as a parallel to that of the phoenix that rises from
its ashes. Here, then, is a water phoenix. . . .
These are facts of the imagination, the very positive
facts of the imaginary world."
— Gaston Bachelard, The Poetics of Space

Sicilians call northerners *polentoni*, because they eat *polenta*, and find them to be without grace.

Fast food: cauldrons of boiled potatoes, roast peppers, and roast onions.

One day I have lunch in the Shangai, a Chinese-red, balconied place above the awnings of La Vucciria; below are the flags and banners of Italy's soccer teams and washed sheets flapping; the food is very bad. *Caponata* — eggplant, capers, and olives in a sweet and sour tomato sauce — is greasy and rancid; but I don't mind, I am snugly enclosed here, above the daily dramas of the bazaar, enjoying public pleasures anonymously.

It is reassuring to see a sign for olives that is as old as the shop, comforting, in a landscape that can often seem apocalyptic, to think that there always have been olives here and there always will be olives here.

Dried aromatic and fetishistic-looking, oregano and basil and mint (an aphrodisiac and an abortifacient, demonic idea) are hung upside down, as witches are. Deep in the recesses of this stall is a shrine to Joseph and Mary and a magnificent set of antlers; perhaps the shopkeeper fears the *cornuto*, the sign of the cuckold, perhaps he fears the evil eye. Ropes of red peppers and garlic surpass the beauty of a baroque fountain in which boys are dunking heads and having a water fight with a blue plastic bucket next to a bas relief of the Spanish tyrant Philip II clasping a serpent to his breast.

Fetishes are everywhere: wax dolls, made to be ex-votos (images to offer God in thanks or supplication for bodily healing), hold flags and soccer balls.

On narrow streets, slippery with refuse, street urchins surround us. We are in the market of the Capo; it is poor. The children — brown and pretty girls with knobby knees and long dark hair — exchange coded signals with one another; their aggression is disguised as sauciness. Or perhaps it is the other way around. If we cannot understand what they want, it is probably because they have not decided what they want, or can reasonably expect to appropriate, from us. There are no boundaries between bodies; perhaps, poor, they sleep many to a bed, they are a tangle of children, and their prodding at our flesh seems natural, a primitive but absolutely reasonable exploration of their environment, which our presence has altered. We have come to find Art Nouveau mosaics on a bakery storefront. And we do (the children tire of their game . . . whatever it was, their game). Sun motes

The women of my family — and most Italian-Americans I know — cook the Sunday tomato sauce for pasta for hours and hours . . . and so, for festive occasions, when we all revert to childhood, willing ourselves to suspend disbelief and remembering only that which was celebratory and good, do I. They call the sauce "gravy," and they call pasta, of whatever variety, "macaronies" (and so, when I am with them, do I). For Christmas I add ground hot and sweet-fennel pork sausage, boneless breasts of chicken cut in strips, beef bracciole, and rolled pork rind stuffed with raisins, pine nuts, parsley, and cheese to the contents of two cans of crushed tomatoes and simmer the sauce for hours. My grandmother Grizzuti cooked this sauce in the basement kitchen of her Brooklyn house on a great black stove. (I attached myself to her apron strings importuning, until she let me dunk stale bread in the iconic liquid.) The pungent fragrance permeated the house and found its way even into the lavender-scented linen closet of the bedroom floor.

Now I like to cook fresh tomatoes for sauce; but when tomatoes in New York taste like cardboard (which they almost always do), I use two

cups of canned plum tomatoes, seeded and
strained, and add a large bunch of fresh basil (the
smaller the leaves the better) and five large cloves
of fresh minced garlic, and a third of a cup of
virgin olive oil, and lots of pepper, and cook
everything all at once for only fifteen minutes. . . .
I learned this recipe from Marcella Hazan.

Sheila, when she is in Rome, serves a warm
pasta with uncooked fresh diced sweet tomatoes of
the kind Italians call marzano, *basil, buffalo*
mozzarella, and panna, *a kind of thick cream we*
don't have in America (lightly whipped heavy
cream can be substituted).

One of my favorite tomato recipes comes from
the original version of Ada Boni's Talisman
Cookbook, *the first Italian cookbook to arrive here*
after World War II, and still in my opinion the best
(Hazan honors Boni by calling her her mentor).
Simmer peeled fresh ripe tomatoes until they
thicken; break eggs into the thick sauce and
scramble them. My children called this egg-and-
tomato rags; it is absolute simplicity.

These beautiful flowers are the blossoms of the homely squash. They are dipped in a flour-and-water batter and fried in vegetable oil. They don't taste as good as they look. Nothing could. Now it is impossible to buy them in New York, they are (like mulberries) too fragile for the marketplace. My grandmothers cultivated them in their Brooklyn backyards; I used to like to wander among the vines that clung to the ground; the trailing vines bore blossom and squash at the same time, which was in contravention of what I knew of nature: a miracle.

PANIFICIO MORELLO
IL CAPO,
PALERMO.

dance in narrow alleys. At the Panificio Morello, we find the object of our search: a brilliant mosaic, an angular stylized woman in gold and lapis lazuli and emerald green; plum-colored chiffon and milky skin in stone. It is aristocratic and denatured, I have a violent reaction to it in this dirty, swarming, yeasty place. It is self-referential art, it needs a context . . .

On the window of the storefront bakery is a poster of just such a pretty girl as those who have been following us: RAPITA, it says.

Men smoke and drink rapaciously and silently and without apparent pleasure in dark, open storefronts, courting oblivion; it is worth a woman's life, to say nothing of her honor, to linger here.

The Belle Epoque came to Palermo with a flowering and a splash: the neoclassical Teatro Massimo (on the steps of which Michael Corleone's daughter meets her death) is just southeast of the Capo. And on Via della Libertà the affinity between chinoiserie (for which the Bourbon kings of Sicily acquired a taste from British merchants of marsala wine and from Lord Nelson) and Art Nouveau (which the Italians call *Liberty*) can be seen in pretty metal kiosks and portes cochere and, to my best delight, in one of the many coffeehouses of that handsome street, Roney — bamboo Liberty fabric on sinuous chairs, and scrolled bamboo screens . . . and *fraises des bois* in clear gelatine, and quivering pink cakes topped with chocolate-studded cream, and *cannoli* (sweetened ricotta cheese in fried tubes) and honey cakes spiced with jasmine, and jellied *nespole* — the small orange Sicilian fruit that is half apricot, half tangerine.

On this street of the *haute bourgeoisie* an aristocratic antique dealer shows us dirty French postcards — girls kissing each other; nymphs (one nipple exposed) cavorting with bears; girls with layers and layers of petticoats straddling each other.

My favorite thing to eat in Palermo is *arancini*, fried golden-orange rice balls stuffed with shredded meat and peas in a spiced tomato sauce, finger food. One day I eat *panelli*, little chick-pea-flour pancakes, with my friend Marialena. The Trattoria Stella — a matter of tables and chairs informally placed, and dripping vines — is in a courtyard in Vecchia Palermo, a neighborhood of many such courtyards, graceful, now *degradato*, dying of bad plumbing, overcrowding, water shortages, and mold, palaces in slums. Marialena looks around, her eyes fill with tears. She remembers. "We danced," she says.

Years of dancing. And no more Belle Epoque villas left; once there were two hundred. We stay at the Villa Igiea Grand, a hotel built in 1900 by the Florios, a great industrial family (who thrive): enfiladed hallways and photographs of kaisers and kings of Siam, Queen Mary (who never looked young), haughty beauties now forgotten; oak staircases and Turkish rugs, milky white Venetian glass, a Roman gazebo near a swimming pool on the sea. At night from my balcony I see in the gardens, amid the almond trees and pines, flashes of white — dinner jackets, and the bare arms of women fanning themselves against the scented heat. Dawn comes, a fire opal, and then pewter skies. An orange sun silences the birds.

In the Liberty dining room, polychromed frescoes of nymphs frivoling innocently and daintily among irises and lilies. On one of the lilies someone has scrawled YO, MARIO! and a phone number.

My favorite place name in Palermo is Via Duca della Verdura — Duke of Vegetable Street.

PALERMO.

Is this a game? Or a rehearsal?
Or a rehearsal and a game?

PALERMO.

*Peasants searched woods, fields, and rivers for
edible greenstuff (wild chicory, wild asparagus,
fennel), and snails and tiny eels with sharp white
teeth that bit their hands, and river crabs, which
they sold from house to house in the poor sections
of Palermo and in the markets; they found frogs,
skinned them, and cut off their heads and feet with
scissors, and broke their legs so they'd look plump.
" 'Even after we've cut off their heads and feet,
skinned them and broken their legs, they still
move,' one man said. . . . 'I often think they're no
different from us. We all eat each other up — you
do, I do. An animal's life is hard as ours.' " They
also sold fresh water in jars, and little vials of
jasmine water.*
— Danilo Dolci, To Feed the Hungry, *1959*

PORTABLE WATER TANK,
PALERMO.

*Drought and the machinations of the Mafia are
held to be responsible for the scarcity of water,
which is available at staggered hours on
staggered days.*

THE CATHEDRAL OF MONREALE,

THE CLOISTER.

Our senses are excited. When we accidentally find ourselves in the suburb of Bagheria (streets in Palermo are ganglions of disrepair), we are revulsed, we roll up the car windows, and we don't know why. We feel that we are in the neighborhood of something repellent. We are: we are driving among grotesques. The crest of the House of Palagonia is a satyr holding up a mirror to a woman with a horse's head. The Villa Palagonia is closed for repairs; we see enough of it to trust Goethe's description of the inside of this malignant house: "The legs of the chairs have been unequally sawn off, so that no one can sit on them; . . . the normal chairs . . . have spikes hidden under their velvet-cushioned seats. . . . A carved crucifix of considerable size . . . is fixed flat to the ceiling. Into the navel of the Crucified a hook has been screwed from which hangs a chain. The end of this chain is made fast to the head of a man, kneeling in prayer. . . . He hangs suspended in the air as a symbol of the ceaseless devotions of the present owner," whose habit it was to beg on the streets of Palermo for alms for the victims of Barbary pirates, who thought of himself as pious and who spent the alms he collected on his hideous house, and who, of course, was mad.

"A confirmed old bachelor by himself has rarely produced anything sensible — witness the case of the Prince of Palagonia — but a celibate group can create the greatest of works." — Goethe.

Five miles southeast of Palermo, in Monreale, is a twelfth-century cathedral combining Moorish and Norman styles. Sober and sumptuous, a discreet blaze of gold: mosaics glorify the walls. Every Bible story you're likely to have heard is depicted here in golden mosaics, amazingly plastic, articulated stone: a po-faced serpent climbs a lollipop tree (an odd thing: perfect Eve's breasts sag); Jesus cures a leper distinguished by his many many spots. Over the panoply of human, animal, and vegetable life broods a huge, majestic, calm, and sturdy Christ.

CAPPELLA PALATINA,

PALERMO.

MOSAIC DETAIL.

Cappella Palatina.
Palermo.

And underneath the cycle of Old and New Testament stories are abstract mosaics, they look like paper-doll cutouts or a child's drawings of Christmas trees.

The cathedral is close with the smell of hothouse lilies and of incense; its baroque *tesoro* (treasury) is close with the smell of human sweat.

In the cloister I do not know whether I am smelling the pale green formal smell of roses or my own perfume. Pigeons burble. Slender columns, no two alike: mosaic bands of black and emerald green and the red of dried blood, and aqua; incised serpents, rams, wise men, grapes, deer, apostles, doves. Within the cloister is a *chiostrina*, a smaller cloister, an enclosure that contains a slender fountain, the water a silken ribbon of light that caresses its shaft; the fountain anchors this corner, the *chiostrina* anchors the cloister, it is perfect psychological space, exciting and safe: a definition of joy? Nothing is single, everything is grouped: grouped in groups of twos.

Above the tiled roofs of the cloister, flowered sheets and men's underwear are hung out to dry.

What is the echo of a fragrance?

What is the color of shade?

In the piazza we have *spremuta d'arancia*, blood-red orange juice with coral foam.

Palermo's Cappella Palatina, in the immense Palazzo dei Normanni, is smaller than the cathedral at Monreale, exquisite. This gold is neither hot nor cold, it creates its own magic climate. I feel like a princess in a garment of gold in a cave of golden stalactites; I would like to be that princess and be married here. Indeed someone *is* being married here; she looks pregnant. If I were the princess of my fantasy I would have as my summer home the nearby deconsecrated church Immanuele, whitewashed, simple, its open door framed with jasmine and roses. From its cloisters I could see the church of San Giovanni degli Eremiti, four red domes on slender white stone pillars: Arabian nights.

CAPPELLA PALATINA.

PALERMO.

MOSAIC DETAIL.

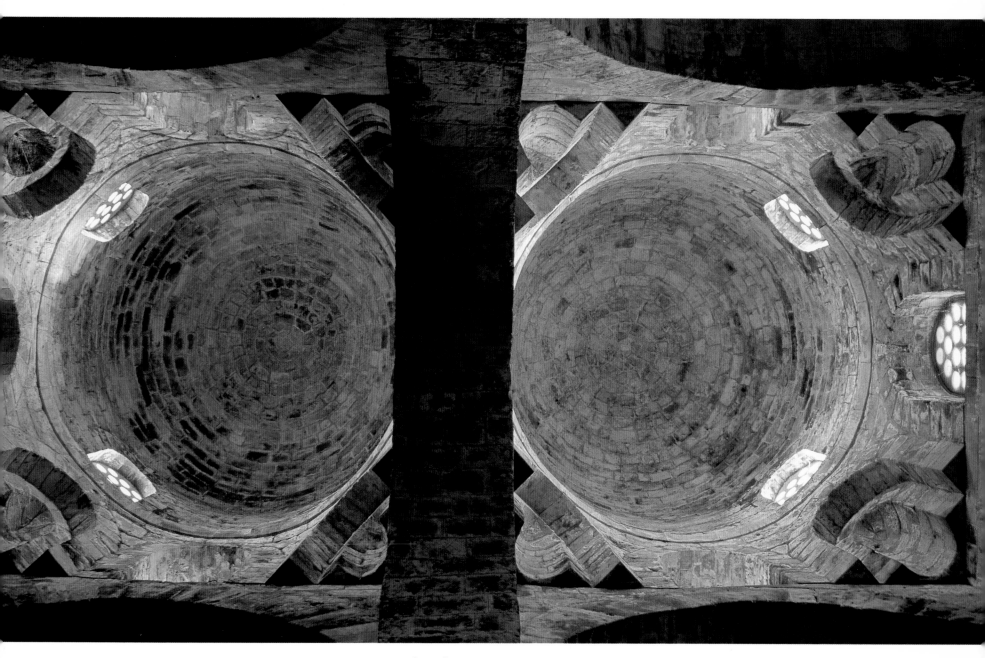

SAN CATALDO,
PALERMO.

Horrors, an underground necropolis: the Capuchin cemetery. They say Velázquez is mummified here, but I couldn't find him, and I don't believe it; why should he be? Eight thousand bodies are mummified here. There's no more room — and no contemporary appetite for this. Guidebooks say the practice of mummifying stopped in the nineteenth century; the pamphlet (bland as bread) distributed by the Capuchin monks says the practice ceased in 1966. Bodies are suspended from the ceiling in crystal boxes, hang (from contraptions like meat hooks) in niches, rot in rotting pine coffins and on rotting shelves, are propped up with bits of twine and penitential rope. In the dry air they are in various stages of decay (during epidemics corpses were dipped in arsenic or lime and then washed with vinegar, but some have been preserved by "secret recipes"). Some have mouths indecently open; their heads rest on cold pillows. Almost all, except for babies (one a malformed fetus, inside organs out), are clothed. They are segregated according to gender, age, and profession.

The clock-maker, amid all the stopped clocks of his shop, places his parchment ear against an out-of-tune grandfather clock; a barber, with dry brush, lathers the cheekbones of an actor learning his role, studying the script with hollow sockets; a girl with a laughing skull milks the carcass of a heifer.

To be sure, many of the living want a fate after death different from their lot in life: the necropolis is crowded with big-game hunters, mezzo-sopranos, bankers, violists, duchesses, courtesans, generals — more than the city ever contained. — Italo Calvino, *Invisible Cities.*

Baron di Portoferrato, 1816–1878, is dressed in his Sulka dressing gown. Shrouds and gloves and business suits and rakish berets and sport shirts and vests and ascots and cummerbunds cover dry skin, yellow bone. What was once a woman sits in a rocker in a flouncy white cap and a pink-and-white morning gown. Grinning. She looks like Anthony Perkins's mother, *Psycho.* Women wearing pretty slippers, their ankles crossed, ribbons, ruffled polka-dot dresses. Babies, their heads bowed, too heavy for their bodies.

My gums begin to bleed.

San Giovanni degli Eremiti, Palermo.

I've always liked the Capuchin cemetery on the Via Veneto in Rome because the monks there arranged bones in artistic rococo patterns on the walls and ceilings; it is an antic, jokey place. I want art as well as faith to mediate between me and death. But Sheila says the Via Veneto is even more obscene; it hides and disfigures the raw truth. This is a nice argument.

Rosalia Lombardo died in 1920, she was a little child. She is perfectly preserved, a yellow ribbon in her abundant auburn hair. People say she looks as if she were sleeping, but this is of course untrue, no art can disguise the absence of a vivifying spark.

Virgins are distinguished from their married sisters by an iron band around their heads, it seems unfair.

It seems unfair that flesh should rot before fabric does.

The Capuchins make jokes. Their long brown garments are spotted and stained. "Don't take too many away from here," they say. "See you soon," they say.

The local fishermen are celebrating a feast day with fireworks; the gold and silver spangles recede just as they seem ready to embrace you with their cold-fire magic, wasted on the summer air. I swim in their reflection in the swimming pool: this is not a miracle you can plan in advance — Busby Berkeley, Esther Williams, Arabian nights.

The lovely coastal road takes us over blue hills, past vineyards that march straight to the sea, past fishing villages and happy beaches, and then we turn inland to Segesta. We climb by car and then arduously on foot to see the great temple where winds congregate and howl as if the massive Doric columns, which seem to take their color from the neighboring golden hills, were a forest of trees. (DON'T WRITE ON CACTUS! says a sign along the road; of course it is ignored: *Johnny loves Maria*. Snails like leeches populate the flesh of cactus plants.) In the forest of columns, birds congregate, too. *Cardinelli*, little black birds with red faces, sing with intense sweetness. They are caught illegally with nets. Young ones fetch $100; unused to captivity, they die. Those bred in cages fetch $300. Naturally everyone who sells a *cardinello* says he bred it in a cage.

A young man is sitting in the deserted temple with his young wife. He has caught a baby bird ("Its parents forget its face when it begins to eat"), and he has placed his *cardinello* in a cage with a black canary. He wants them to mate, he wants to make a "miracle." He has constructed the cage so as to hide the female bird from the male. "When they don't see each other they sing," he says, "like Frank Sinatra. Only the male sings." The young man and his wife are childless, and poor.

The sea is visible, a blue crease, from this lonely height.

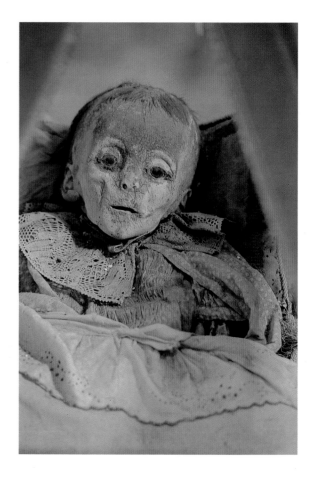

Capuchin cemetery,
Palermo.

*"What a great principle of humanity burial is,
imagine a feral state in which the human bodies
remain unburied on the surface of the earth as food
for crows and dogs. Certainly this bestial custom
will be accompanied by uncultivated fields and
uninhabited cities. Men will go about like swine
eating the acorns found amidst the putrefaction of
their dead. And so with good reason burials were
characterized by the sublime phrase 'compacts of
the human race,' . . . and with less grandeur were
described by Tacitus as 'fellowships of humanity.' "*
— The New Science of Giambattista Vico, *1744,*
translated by Thomas Goddard Bergin and
Max Harold Fisch

On the coastal road we passed Trapani; and in its industrial suburbs windmills, out of place, out of time — stout towers, lacy arms — and salt flats. Three thievish-looking men from an iron works took us to the flats, we were lost. We waited on the side of the road for the sun to set, for the salt water to turn red. The bamboo rustled like torn silk. I saw a driver steer his car with one hand and hold the reins of his horse, who was cantering along the road, with the other. The light slowly changed; the silence, not passive but active, absorbed — contained — all sound. Like Shiva, dancing forever his silent dance. Silence is the garment of light. The quiet water, heavy with salt, turns lavender, orange, Persian melon, amber: the colors of exotic fruit, of shot silk, of an oriental potentate, of Kublai Khan. And the salt is an underglaze; I stare into silvered mirrors.

We climb to the hills, the sea always with us, curving toward us no matter what direction the curling road takes. Goats and cows graze above the clouds. The sun is bright, there is a cool breeze, the oleander and geraniums are intensely colored, invigorated by the mountain air. Bells sound in the swirling mists. We spend the night in Erice, 2,000 feet above the sea — we can see Tunisia from here — the mythical home of Eryx Astarte, Venus.

   D. H. Lawrence said that Erice made his "darkness quiver"; it didn't mine. Englishmen have

SALT FLATS,

TRAPANI.

great affection for Erice; they like to think it is a medieval town, which it is, but not noticeably. Winds exercise brute force around corners. What is underfoot is lovely — satiny steps in winding alleys and in tunnels — and what is above eye level is lovely — ancient lintels and tiled roofs. For the rest, it is gray low houses, hidden courtyards, tourist kitsch. Maybe, Sheila says, Englishmen like it here because it is the perfect setting for a mystery, for Sherlock Holmes. One thinks of assassinations here, of daggers pointed as pointed smiles. I think the English love it here because it is foggy. And clean. The satin cobblestones are treacherous. The mountain falls sharply, exhausted, into the sea. The smell of new-mown hay is intensified by mists, it mingles with the iodine smell of the sea, and — so high above it — I can taste the sea.

Temples should always be placed near the surge and sound of the persuasive sea. In Selinunte (which takes its name from the Greek word for wild celery, *selinon*) it is easy to believe that the mighty ancient ruins were always honey-gold. They were not; they were once brazen red and chalk white and black, fun-house colors. The other buildings on this site are jumbly heaps of unreconstructed stone that the eye and mind cannot decipher without the aid of an exhibition at the little museum on the site of the excavations, where the story of this doomed architecture is told by means of little bits of cork. Only the temple remains — its spongy tufa stone looks like cork — and its "timelessness" is the result of technology.

You have to make up stories in your head about these ruins or else empty your head completely and rely on telepathic images. Tourists ease their bodies out of buses, so hot, so tired. They make a choked and sliding *aaahhh* sound, a musical grunt.

On the road to Agrigento, sheep look like rocks and rocks look like sheep and we never see shepherds, who hide.

ERICE.

*"The city . . . does not tell its past, but contains it
like the lines of a hand, written in the corners of
the streets, the gratings of the windows, the
banisters of the steps, the antennae of the lightning
rods, the poles of the flags, every segment marked
in turn with scratches, indentations, scrolls."*
— *Italo Calvino*, Invisible Cities

Selinunte.

My hotel is an eighteenth-century villa on the sea; and from my terrace I can see the Temple of Concord, beautifully preserved — immense, its authority an immense surprise. Old olive trees and vineyards and lime trees and cypresses (and a swimming pool surrounded by mock-Polynesian straw umbrellas) separate me from the temple on its elevated slope. I am content to look at it — no dusty browsing among temples in the heat. A member of the visiting Virgilian Society asks me to tour the Valley of the Temples with him; but I do not want to share the moonlight. Near the temple is a graveyard, old; the temple, ancient, is much more vivacious. At night the temple is illuminated (I swim); but in any light it looks as if the light is emanating from *it*, as if what is bleeding from the sky is absorbed in it and has for centuries found a home in it.

Sheep graze under the olive trees.

A bride stands in her wedding dress, a vulgar, tiered affair, amusing against the awesome severity of the temple (she gives no offense).

The wind blows hard and hot at night. It stops at the threshold of my balcony door. The mosquitoes don't mind it. Hot, sweaty, eaten alive. And the temple lighted and oblivious.

I hear a happy (juiced) Virgilian: I AM NOT IN NEW JERSEY! he shouts, fervor swinging his words up toward the sky.

The Agrigento Tourist Agency has offered couples "in crisis" — couples who have applied for divorce — a free weekend at a hotel; this will accomplish, they appear to think, "the renaissance of love." Not if the mosquitoes bite.

The temples play peekaboo as we drive. They appear, they disappear, now you see them, now you don't. How can such great things be coy?

We pass through a town where a judge has just been shot; two men were shot in Agrigento after we left; we pass through little Pietraperzia, where three people have just been shot, two of them killed. The Mafia no longer obeys its own rules: in recent killings they have indiscriminately attacked and shot wives and fiancées, noncombatants.

In the inland town of Caltagirone it is 115 degrees. (The only kingdom I want is the Kingdom of Cool.) A toothless man, so old only his clothes declare his gender — layered sweaters and a corduroy suit — sells day-old newspapers from a cardboard box suspended by a horseshoe rope of plastic around his neck. Like a cigarette girl. His hand is very cold.

The gardens are dusty.

Dour men in purposeless clusters stand in the piazza before noon. There is nothing for them to do. Counting the cobblestones. Each is wrapped in torpid solitude. Maximum unemployment, maximum heat, maximum despair.

AGRIGENTO.

Caltagirone is famous for its stairs, the Scala di Santa Maria del Monte, 142 of them, every riser adorned with yellow, blue, and white ceramic tiles in patterns that date back to the tenth century, very gay.

Nothing on earth could convince me to walk up or down those steps, I am vertiginous just looking at them, they stretch up and up, on and on. A dentist who doubles as a plastic surgeon has hung his shingle out on a landing of the stairs: double trouble, stairs and root canal. But Sheila doesn't see it that way; she likes to climb the steps, which she calls pleasant. Children play on them, old people pause on them, each is two feet wide.

A saucy boy in blue stands with a blue soccer ball on top of the blue, yellow, and white stairs; he poses with his chin thrust out.

On feast days wicks are placed in antique-paper cups on terra-cotta bases, thousands of cups are placed on the stairs (this was the idea of a Benedictine). The cups are painted red and green and white. When they are lit, they make a design that goes all the way up the steps. Each year the design is changed depending on the placement of the cups; sometimes it is abstract, sometimes representational. Every year since 1927 it has been the work of one man, Don Cicciono Russo. A whistle blows promptly at 9:30 P.M., and four thousand oil lights

shine; I have not seen this, I cannot imagine it: flames of fire and the shadows of a fiery design on walls of the sad houses that line the terrible steps.

When we ask directions of the *vigili* they salute us and lead us in their cars to our destination, so kind.

Vespers in the church of Santa Maria del Monte. Women in the church. (Men in the piazza.) Their singing is too full of vivid yearning to be despair, too mournful to be hope, too *allegra* to be resignation — faith that sees but doesn't see how. Their solace is implicit in their sorrow.

In this terrible town in a bleak hotel we had an antipasto of grilled eggplant dressed in fresh tomato sauce; marinated squid; pickled red onions; kidney beans with oil and lemon and oregano; roasted peppers, green, yellow, red. Then *occhi di lupo*, short tubular macaroni with sweet tomato sauce and basil; grilled swordfish with oil and lemon; chocolate and strawberry ice cream. We drank peach nectar with mineral water.

All day long in Caltagirone we hear the music from *Staying Alive*.

CALTAGIRONE.

Medieval/baroque hilly Ragusa Ibla. Stone grotesques support stone balconies, fat tongues loll obscenely between fat, pendulous lips and feral pointed teeth; stone men with hooked noses like birds' beaks and furry faces like those of animals. Sweet clean mountain air and thirty-two churches.

Four formal old men, jackets draped on old bones, legs like twigs, sit in a row in front of a cafe talking of marvels past. They are discussing whether the baron is at home. "These people, they can't leave us alone," they say. They mean us. They mean women. We have moved an empty table and sit half in and half out of a tunneled street, half in and half out of shade, nice. The proprietress of the cafe cultivates a sad geranium that will not root. A priest buys apricots from a truck in front of a deserted palazzo; the fruit seller is dressed in madras shorts, white socks, and sandals, he sings the Mad Song from *Lucia di Lammermoor*. In the lifetime of the old men the population of old Ibla has gone from 17,000 to 4,000; Ibla doesn't have its own mayor now. But the princess still comes, they assure us, there is a disco in a palazzo. The old men have gotten used to our presence, they want to tell us their lives. Their lives tell this story: bureaucrats are little better than the feudal aristocrats whose departure the old men see as betrayal, it has brought them ruin.

We want to see a deserted palazzo, we invent a friend, a rich American industrialist who wants to buy a palace with twenty-five rooms. The old men heave their creaking bones onto Vespas and roar away in all directions, ties flapping in the wind, to find the *padrone* of the palazzo. We have made their day (they have made ours).

We gain entrance to the courtyard: flowering cacti in tubs, a double flight of steps. We knock on the heavy door. No one answers. The *portiere* confronts us, glowering, we are the Enemy: it will take

millions for your rich American to evict us, he says; he rents a store on the ground level of the palace. The old men spit.

A man walks by, he is the image of a gargoyle on a balcony.

On the *autostrada* there is a roadblock sign. Not one driver pays it any mind. We think it is a way of foxing us (we have caught the Sicilian habit of distrusting all authority), to what end we can only guess. Eight cars play follow-the-blind-leader. We come, just as the road sign warned, to a dead end, and we must detour now for miles. We can read the thoughts of the driver ahead of us in a white van, his outstretched hand in eloquent gestures reveals his mind:

Why did they do this? Stupid, and where do we go now? Ah, well, life is like that. And look at the people behind us, fools like us.

Sheila's husband, Giuseppe, says that no man who drives wearing a hat is a good driver, and he is right.

On the way to Noto tongues of fire ignite spontaneously near dry walls that are incoherently placed, this in an arid landscape that has no logic. Everything that grows is gallant. The fire spins itself into a fury: dervishes of fire accompany us for miles.

In the spring, blankets of flowers are woven to cover the streets of Noto, a city of golden Sicilian baroque, brazenly theatrical . . . and, ravaged by earthquakes and time, falling to pieces, shored up, like those pictures one sees of Noah's Ark, on wooden supporting ramps — but not so likely to survive a deluge. Noto is a dream of what Noto once was . . . might have been . . . may be again — provisional, all netting and bulwarks and scaffolding, existing in limbo, in a kind of stasis that contradicts the restless spirit of the baroque. A city on the cusp between death and rebirth. Weeds sprout. Atlantis: a golden city dying before one's

"Marriage . . . is a chaste carnal union consummated under the fear of some divinity, . . . defined among the Romans as omnis vitae consortium, *a lifelong sharing of lot, and the husband and wife were called* consortes, *or lot sharers. And to this day Italian girls when they marry are said to take up their lot,* prender sorte.*"*
— *Giambattista Vico*

NOTO;

SWEETS.

In The Leopard, *Lampedusa describes the sweet*
course of an aristocratic banquet during the
Garibaldi era: "Huge blond babas, Mont Blancs
snowy with whipped cream, cakes speckled with
white almonds and green pistachio nuts, hillocks
of chocolate-covered pastry, brown and rich as the
topsoil of the Catanian plain from which, in fact,
through many a twist and turn they had come,
pink ices, champagne ices, coffee ices, all parfaits,
which fell apart with a squelch as the knife cleft
them, melody in major of crystallized cherries,
acid notes of yellow pineapple, and those cakes
called 'triumphs of gluttony,' filled with green
pistachio paste, and shameless 'virgins' cakes'
shaped like breasts." . . . When my brother and I
were growing up in Brooklyn, where the Italian
pastries rival those of Sicily, we called all ices
lemon-ice, we thought that was their generic name:
"Could I have a chocolate lemonice, please?"

eyes. A city of jumbled metaphors that mocks one's
attempt to make sense of it: restoration and decay.
At night one is almost able (intermittently) to
believe that its gold is not false coin: the Duomo
glimpsed through branches of a monkey-puzzle tree
(three old men sitting on green plastic chairs in front
of it).

I find the Noto I will remember on Via Ducce-
zio: the concave, rococo, confectionary church of
Santa Maria del Carmine, which embraces you, and
a restaurant called Carmine, and the Pasticceria
Mandolfiore, in which the confections are rococo
and baroque, as exuberant as poor Noto is not.

Carmine's proprietor wears two wedding
bands, his, and that of his wife, recently dead. He
has three boys and three grown daughters and any
mention of anything that remotely pertains to their
mother sets the women crying. They cry as they
serve us dressed in black. One sees the daughters'
futures clearly: sacrificial lives, forever black.

They do what they do in spite of all: we have an
exquisite rabbit casserole, the rabbit sautéed in
olive oil and cooked in white wine and the red wine
vinegar that they make, a *soffritto* of carrots and
mint and olives and capers and white wine brought
together with the rabbit at the end of cooking (the
surprise is in the mint).

We look at many snapshots of the couple's fiftieth wedding anniversary; Carmine offers us his
ocean villa for the season; and I wonder, as I have
wondered often on this island: where is the fabled
Sicilian reserve?

(And I wonder as I have wondered before: if I
could understand why Sicily is in love with its own
grotesques and its dark caves, would I have the key
to Sicily?)

The Pasticceria Mandolfiore presents us with
onerous choices: *cassata* iced with lime ice cream;
vanilla ice cream flecked with chocolate and stud-

ded with citron and candied cherries (buried
treasure, jewels); strawberry *cassata* with chocolate
pips; marzipan: corn, figs, mandarins (deliberately
and artistically flawed), marzipan cakes of Lux soap
(it is a joke told against the Sicilians that when Garibaldi gave them soap they thought it was cheese
and ate it; and this is their retaliatory joke, a nice
last word); ricotta ice cream (ricotta, milk, and
sugar) in conical bamboo-and-straw containers,
scaled-down versions of those the cheese comes in
(these are made by old people who might otherwise
have nothing with which to occupy their hands);
marzipan sacred hearts and curly-haired white
lambs; meringues and peach-and-cream ice cream
in pastry peaches (with sugar-fuzz — the Sicilians
take this business seriously; these confections are
made in a place that is called a laboratory). Ephem-
eral art.

Ex-votos made of bread: eyes of dough (for
Santa Lucia, patroness of sight); lungs and hands of
dough; buns of San Biaggio, patron of the trachea.

Ciambelle i cudduri — giant doughnuts decorated with pasta snakes, protection against
snakebite.

On the Feast of the Dead, November 2, children are given grapes and suns and moons and
thighbones made of sugar.

Conceptual art.

"If you ask, 'Why is . . . construction taking
such a long time?' the inhabitants . . . answer, 'So
that its destruction cannot begin.' And if asked
whether they fear that, once the scaffoldings are
removed, the city may begin to crumble and fall to
pieces, they add hastily, in a whisper, 'Not only the
city.'" — Italo Calvino, *Invisible Cities*.

ENNA.

CALTAGIRONE.

"A melting light embracing memory, distance,
indefinable tenderness."
— *Leonardo Sciascia*, The Wine-Dark Sea

PORTOPALO.

The mosquitoes. Insect repellent rots my fingernail polish but does not repel the mosquitoes.

There are concrete bunkers on the sea, and Fascist pleasure palaces the Fascists had no time to finish. Notwithstanding which, this coast, south of Noto, is beautiful, and fecund: watermelons, grapevines, tomatoes; crystal water, miles of empty beaches.

We are farther south than Tunis, and it is cloudless, it almost never rains.

In Roman times, *pali* (poles) rose from this water to signal the arrival of pirates and invaders. (A ferocious pirate called Mohammed Dagut the Turk is used to keep Sicilian children in line, as we use the bogeyman — such a long history the Sicilians have to keep alive, their faces are lined with memories of memories.) And later watchtowers rose, from which, on July 10, 1943, the invading Allies could be seen.

On the southeastern tip of Sicily, in Portopalo, we find a hotel of sumptuous second-rate public rooms: gilt and velvet chairs dangerous to sit upon, majolica, fake forsythia and orchids, paintings of squinty-eyed saints and one-armed paladins and bilious cardinals. In the early nineteenth century one Baron Rau Xa Xa, a Palermitano of Spanish origin, built a palace next to a tuna factory; from the Castello in which we stay — the folly of Prince Bruna di Belmonte, who built it in 1915 for his bride, the princess of Monte Carlo, a thing of ramparts and parapets and oil lamps and winding stairs and useless halls that lead to blank walls — we can see the old palace and the dilapidated tuna factory.

The Castello is a comfortable joke; its courtyard is a pasha's dream. Sheets of bougainvillea cascade over a central well; children know enough to pose here innocent in white.

There is a wedding at the Castello, she pale and pearly, candid and ardent, he shiny and squat and sweet. Baby carriages and old people fill the banquet hall. Prosciutto with pineapple; tortellini with spinach and ricotta; a pork roast and a beef roast; two vegetables; sherbet; green salad; a seven-layer cake made with custard and orange water and Chantilly cream, a replica of the Castello. Awed by all this food, I have delicate cauliflower for dinner, and a delicate white wine with the faintest hint of jasmine.

The wedding favors are plastic dolls. Turn the doll around, and underneath the pedestal on which she stands you see a sherbet-pink plastic baby, fetal.

The morning sky is too wonderful, sunrise is kitschy, a painting on velvet; a thousand birds scissor and skid across the face of a red sun that makes a rosy path on pulsing waters to my door, a fishing boat cuts across the path; atop a ruined castle a lighthouse sends forth a watery beam.

The bride and groom come down to breakfast, it is touching how glad we all are to see them, as if they might have gotten lost during the night; they are wearing bedroom slippers.

The fishermen are mending their nets, sober work, delicate work, patient work. I feel tender toward them; their gnarled fingers, their silence.

After noon the fishing boats come in, fish is auctioned on white tile slabs, a private rite in a public place, incomprehensible words fluid and fast as rushing waters, foreign gestures, a cult, a temple of bloody fish. Cuttlefish and squid, lobster and swordfish and sea bass and *gamberoni;* fish with golden eyes; wrinkled, black-spotted coral fish with fanlike tails and gills, ugly and elegant, like Diana Vreeland. The eels are orphaned, nobody buys them, they are so fresh their eyes, amazed and alert, look as if they contain a live and lively intelligence. The fishermen are paunchy as if, tired of fish, they eat olives and bread and pasta and meat and cream. They eat sweet buns and drink sweet coffee in the trattoria on the docks.

For dinner I have smoked swordfish garnished with the orange pulp of sea urchins.

A Venetian of severe beauty is sitting with her lover on the terrace under an orange moon. She is drinking almond nectar from Avola, a drink like crushed pearls. Happiness has made him raucous; he is arguing that the fish auctioneers start with high prices and then go down, she that the auction works the other way around, from low prices to high; this is love play. Next they quarrel over whether the market has fresh buffalo mozzarella on Tuesday, this is serious business. She says that the reason there are no gardens in Portopalo is that it was for the grand *seigneur* to have gardens, not the *contadini,* this is a legacy from feudalism. Besides, she says, why bother, when left to itself the earth will sprout in its own time and way, trust it — and the Sicilians are clusters of flowers, she says, they live in the open. She comes to Portopalo for "a little bit of Africa," she says . . . and because her first husband was Sicilian.

There is a poetry Italians tell. We say the names of towns we love. *Aaah, Luccignano!* the Venetian says. There is silence; and then we sigh. We are inwardly rehearsing all the reasons for our love; we are brought together by diverse memories unspoken.

Near Portopalo, unmarked on the map, is a nature and wildlife reserve, Vendicari. "We make love there," the Venetian's lover says, she kicks him gently with a long, elegantly shod foot (too practiced to blush).

The road ends a kilometer from the white sand beach. I walk past unworked salt flats, crystals oddly dull but palely magical under the morning sun. And then past a marsh and then a swamp which adds a not unpleasant undertone of overripe decaying vegetable matter to the frank sweet fragrance of ripe strawberries. White butterflies among raspberry canes; whispering papyrus. The air is delicious, this is a still delirium. There is no one making love on the beach. Far away there is a tableau: a fat baby, back to the sea, tearing up his picture book while fond parents look on. I walk another kilometer into the sea before my shoulders are immersed in water. Paradise enough to make one wish Eve hadn't eaten the apple. The Ionian meets the Mediterranean here, it is like a friendly turquoise pond. The warm safe waters are so clear; I see my friendly feet. A fisherman gives me a lift back to the main road. His car smells of sweat, tuna, and beer. On his bare chest are tattooed the words: VIVA LA MALAVITA! — Long Live the Mafia!

I am in a restaurant on the waterfront and I am crying. I don't know why I am crying. Suddenly I do; memory has sprung a tender trap: Over twenty years ago I sat in this very place with my children, two and three. (How could I have forgotten. These days I don't set my mind the task of remembering my children's infancy, I am never sure whether the pain I feel when I peel back the years belongs to them or to me; one can understand one's own pain and how one has earned it — one can trace the genealogy of one's pain; but the pain of others is unbearable because it is obscure, each life is a mystery, dread accompanies the contemplation of it.) Twenty years ago we sailed from Bombay to New York, stopping here in Siracusa . . . Stopping first in Suez, where a black-robed magician put a coin in my daughter's hand that changed into a yellow bird . . . I saw this happen. The hooli-booli man he was called. So then in Siracusa, my daughter, Anna, pointed at every black-robed priest she saw: "Is he the hooli-booli man?" she asked. Perhaps the reason Anna studies theology is that a base coin turned into a golden bird in her hand and when we lit candles in the cathedral of Siracusa she thanked the hooli-booli man, believing him to be part of the same magic. (Perhaps when I am a grandmother I will set my mind the task of remembering my children's infancy. . . . Everyone in Sicily my age is a grandmother!)

Those years ago, in this very port, a country woman dressed all in black fell to her knees in horror and in prayer when she spied me, because I was wearing slacks . . . though one would have thought, my arms being full of babies, she might have found me acceptable — how things have changed. Not that Siracusa isn't witchy anymore. . . .

In the vicinity of the port is the Fountain of Arethusa — a kind of tank, a square enclosure of sweet water near the salt of the sea. Pursued by the river god Alpheus in Arcadia, the nymph Arethusa begged Artemis, the goddess of virginity, to save her; Artemis obliged by turning her into a river, and as a river she fled from Arcadia to Sicily and surfaced here, in this fountain, where the waters of the pursued and the pursuer mingle. (We are not told whether they were happy thus; happiness seems not to be the point of Greek myths.) The fountain is surrounded by papyrus, very elegant, and infested with swans (monogamous and cruel); the graceful birds stand on their heads in the water; they sit, like domestic cats, on haunches one didn't know they had.

The cathedral is a five-minute walk from the port (which is in the old city of Ortigia, joined to the modern mainland by two bridges; we eschew the nervous and ugly modern mainland). Kind women stop us: Watch your purse, your purse! they say; bad boys are here, they say. But I can't work up any fear. (After all, my children once were here.) The lanes of Ortygia are dark and narrow but they are unthreatening. We can see into the courtyards where the Ortygians (like the Milanesi) live; the life of courtyards dissipates fears, life is just beyond one's footfalls, all around one.

Grotesques sag under the weight of ruined baroque balconies. . . . We walk. . . .

PORTOPALO.

And then — the bliss — cathedral square. *Granita!* Privacy achieved in public, the bliss! This square is handsome enough for cardinals. And accommodating: in the boat-shaped, oleander-lined piazza, black Moroccans in long white dresses walk hand in manly hand; cheeky boys in shorts manipulate remote controls — their toy Maseratis scoot under the feet of dogs who play a mating game; a couple quarrels unselfconsciously (she in a flowered dress and slippers): they have brought their quarrel out into this public living room to which *cortili*, courtyards, are an anteroom. Girls in golden sandals. *Froci* boys, their pinkies linked. A beribboned little girl in pajamas taking her first steps. Tourists. Lovers. *Carabinieri* in blinding white shirts. Vespas. "I have so missed a piazza," Calvino wrote when he was a long time without one, and so have I, I want to be a sedentary tourist, breakfast in the piazza, and lunch, and ices, dinner, newspapers, safely observing, safely observed.

Where does one go for solitude in a city? To a square.

Opposite the cathedral the square widens. The buildings facing the cathedral are almost imperceptibly concave, a discreet gesture of homage to the Duomo, which is an example of architectural Darwinism, it has evolved from the ruins of a temple of Athena; Doric columns remain (a lovely skeleton) in the Norman interior, their austerity enhanced by the baroque façade. A friendly church . . . a neighborhood church.

Somewhat guiltily I went to the Archeological Park on the mainland to see the ruins of Greek altars and theaters; I had grown weary of antiquities, I longed for the life of the squares. I'd had enough of stone stoniness, blossoms in the dust, capers growing from the ruins, citrus groves heavy with the scent of fallen fruit decaying among decaying stone. I stayed to see the caverns and the caves; a cave, man's first home, and, perhaps, his last, promises both protection and obliteration, it is a dicey refuge from the living storm. There is an artificial grotto in the park, no one knows why it was built. Hundreds of doves make it their home (well; so long as bats do not). No guarantees: twenty-three meters high, the grotto reaches upward into darkness and stretches forward into darkness; its mouth is a series of sensual folds that Caravaggio, we are told, christened "the ear of Dionysius" — why? He must have seen in the forms of the grotto the lips of a vagina, and a womb, he was a sensualist, he loved women. Ah, but love of women coexists with terror of the womb, the catacomb from which we reach out and into our little lives.

The Grotta dei Cordari, nearby, is another matter: one sees the end from the beginning, the sunlight reaches the magnolia leaves at this cave's entrance from the other side. And that lessens the terror . . . also the thrill.

THE BELVEDERE AT
CALASCIBETTA.

*"Everything beyond a certain distance is dark, and
yet everything is full of being around us."*
— *Teilhard de Chardin*, The Divine Milieu

I have been reading Giuseppe di Lampedusa, *The Leopard*, a book so beautiful, wise, and melancholy I can bear even (almost) the mosquitoes. I find a cemetery where — this is odd but (I don't know why) not alarming — I see on tombstones the names I have been reading in Lampedusa's novel. I am happy here, where hollyhocks — a most unmordant flower — grow.

Calvino said that when his spirit needed music he found it in the cemeteries: "The musicians hide in the tombs; from grave to grave flute trills, harp chords answer one another." We go to cemeteries to court an understanding life, to decipher our own names on the stone slabs of the dead: "Like the city of the living, this other city communicates a history of toil, anger, illusions, emotions; only here all has become necessary, divorced from chance, categorized, set in order." We go for communion and for explanations; we understand that the explanations will be partial, inconclusive. We go because melancholy is the soil from which wisdom grows. We go because there is safety in the city of the dead, there is order. We go to honor our contract with the dead, without which there is no civilization — we hold them in our minds, with love. We go to escape anxiety, terror. We go because we do not wish to die and know we must.

Plastic-reproduction pietàs, and bleeding hearts, and gratuitous ceramic flowers. This is love, though not as I would express it. The grave of Cecilia Bongiovanni, 1883–1956, is still visited: fresh gladioli rest against her tomb. I smile at the dead who smile at me from the photographs on their headstones. Outside the gates boys play soccer.

Skulls and bones; and in empty drawer number 8 — the dead are stacked in marble drawers when they are not housed in Norman, Arabic, or Gothic mausoleums — there is Windex and detergent. The fruit-and-vegetable man is selling cherries outside the gate.

This cemetery is on a belvedere, it overlooks the world.

In town I buy a white nightgown with fine lace and pearl buttons.

In the town of Calascibetta there is another belvedere that overlooks the world, the world is pearly gray and infinite. It is dusk. Three men stand at the edge of a precipice looking past fields of tawny stubble to blue hills, they are old, their eyes are milky. What they see on the horizon is different from what I see on the horizon. Below them is a garden. This garden is on top of the world, it springs from ash-gray earth, it is surrounded by rocks and it grows from the foundations of a gutted medieval building. In this garden bordered with old tiles there is a fig tree; cabbages; roses; basil; hollyhocks. The land is good; but there is not enough water. I can smell the basil. Even in times of drought there is a garden. My maternal grandfather was a stern, sometimes a brutal man; but no one grew vegetables as knowingly and as tenderly as he, he planted peppers and tomatoes in the backyard of a tenement. The tenement smelled of wine, old age, and virile despair. The garden, where he wrapped a fig tree in tar paper and crowned it with a metal pail to shield it from the winds of winter, smelled of light. The day before he died he harvested his garden.

These gardens recognize no hierarchy of values, peppers grow next to gladioli. These gardens are like memory: whatever is in them belongs in them and is exactly right.

Lampedusa smells a French rose and it reminds him of the thigh of a French dancer.

I am thinking of the small of a man's back, the nape of a man's neck (I once had a lover about whom I loved nothing but the yeasty smell of him). The landscape is sensual, varied, intricate, romantic, undulating. Summer; the wheat and fava beans are harvested: chocolate swatches, golden fields. The hills are scooped, sculpted, folded; nature abhors a straight line. Like ribbons of cake batter, chocolate cake, yellow cake, someone says; how not to take one's metaphors from food? Tender green sprouts in the dark brown earth that we call chocolate. An impeccably beautiful abstraction that keeps all the rules . . . like a good abstract expressionist painting. The viewer may not know the rules but the painting does and is true to them; what looks arbitrary is ordered. Like the desert petrified, someone says. (I want to run my hands over it . . . over the small of his back, the nape of his neck . . .) Like a sea petrified, Lampedusa says, "conceived apparently in a delirious moment of creation . . . aridly undulating . . . comfortless and irrational with no lines that the mind [can] grasp"; he doesn't love it. Ahead there are rocky hills — velvet, but true to their rockiness. I am warm and lazy and exalted, a child making sand castles, the sand yielding to my hand, my mind is a hand.

A Franciscan climbs out of a red Fiat.

A mule drinks from the long baroque trough of Leonforte, a fountain that has twenty-four spouts that supply twenty-four meager arches of water. The fountain trough is the color of the hills and the hills are the color of the mule driver's face.

A man with a paunch and a scar knocks bales of hay from the roof of his car with a chartreuse plastic cane. He asks us to take his picture. He gets a camera from the back of his car. It is carefully wrapped in butcher paper, and it comes to us that the camera has been stolen, but we snap his picture anyway . . . even though his camera has no film. We snap and snap and he strikes poses.

We are surrounded by henna-colored bulls. Their horns brush the window of our car; a bull kicks our fender. The shepherd doesn't care. He is lethargic. The bulls are too.

Italians all love their towns and cities. When a place is boring they call it tranquil; this is an adorable characteristic; but sometimes it is misleading.

In Enna, the center and belly of Sicily, we stop at a light to consult a map, and a man with an imperfect mustache and moist eyes approaches us, he looks as if unclothed he would be the consistency of lumpy mashed potatoes. He wears ill-assorted clothes too heavy for the weather. Are-you-from-Springfield-I-am-the-descendant-of-a-baron, he says. His face is glistening with earnestness and with sweat. He is from a family of artists, he is a typographer, he says. His sister is an architect, she lives south of here on the Lake of Pergusa (where Pluto abducted Persephone, the goddess of Spring);

LEONFORTE.

CALASCIBETTA.

the lake is caked mud, dry, his sister is unmarried. He, Rudolfo, is unmarried too, and on account of this aggrieved. He invites us to his sister's house for dinner. We go with him to a cafe, courtesy (and curiosity) require it. We have the best water in the world in Enna, he says; money means nothing when you have peace in your soul, he says; we are all brothers, he says . . . and he says all of this *sotto voce*, as if his boring words could cause a conflagration. He looks around nervously to see if we are being observed; he wants to be observed/he doesn't want to be observed. Not all is perfect even here in Italy, he says (whispering): *The Mafia. The Mafia has a stranglehold on us, all these buildings are Mafia buildings, washed money. You have to know someone to live.* He fidgets, his arm touches mine too often. He draws strength from his *caffè corretto*, espresso with *grappa*. He tells us proudly that the Mafia has, from time to time, come to his aid . . . and after another *caffè corretto*, he tells us he is a made man, "a man of honor." He says this in a loud voice, drawing icy glances from the men in the cafe, over whom a sodden silence falls, whereupon we decide that we must leave. He leaves us knowing that he will be disappointed in us; he casts a reproachful glance as we retreat.

He is a hungry man standing with his nose pressed against the bakery window. In him are mingled reproachfulness, a sense of entitlement, generosity, shame, bewilderment, dogmatism, fear, bravado, candor, duplicity. (He wears a Cross around his neck, and a gold dogtag engraved with his blood type; he doesn't believe in the Cross; he doesn't believe in taking chances.) It is not possible to think of him as "a man of honor," a Mafia soldier; a made man is a man of spiritual sloth and existential cowardice, but also a man of apparent courage, worldly virility, a man with presence and self-assurance, a bold man, a man to be reckoned with. *Omertà* — a manliness that is expressed in silence — does not belong to Rudolfo.

In the medieval town of Nicosia a drunk man in a cowboy hat informs us that he is mayor and policeman; we dodge, he follows, a pest. Another man sends the Nicosian cowboy on his way and approaches us tentatively, solemnly, with a southern tenderness of manner, and gravity. This man's name is Fiore, flower. With apologies for his imperfect English — "I used to read" — he tells us his story, a Sicilian story. He is tied to this small town by ties of duty, affection, and lassitude. He apologizes for being fat, for being old (fifty), for taking up our time — but his manner is so ironic as to avoid making an appeal to our pity. He wants not to be regarded as a supplicant. He tells us a story dammed up for years; it is because we are sympathetic passing strangers that he can hand his story over to us, we will carry it away with us.

For many years Fiore edited an Italian newspaper in Australia, he visited China, Japan, Los Angeles, New York, he felt himself to be a man of the great world. He returned to little Nicosia seventeen times in twenty years; when he was thirty-four he married, here, a teacher, a woman he adored.

His son, Nicolo, has forgotten how to speak English; Fiore has been in Nicosia for five years, and he has spoken English only three times, this is the fourth. . . . "I will tell my son never to marry." . . . He adores nine-year-old Nicolo with the fervor he once reserved for his wife, "still beautiful."

Fiore came back to Nicosia because his father was dying of cancer; in fact his father is alive and well, he smokes five packs of cigarettes a day. Fiore's mother pays him a weekly allowance to augment the money he gets from renting his flat in Sydney, a bribe to keep him here. Whenever he says that he will leave this town where everybody knows everybody else's business, she falls on her knees and prays. You don't believe in God, you don't love me, she says. He loves her. She is afraid of the old-age home.

He has no work. His wife's family says: Why not be a bricklayer? "They tell her how to arrange the furniture, they watch every move. If you go to a pharmacy they think you have a lover. It is all finished between us, we make love three times a week, we both need love, but not from each other. Her stream of love has run dry." He manages to say all this without indelicacy. He has no friends in town, the townsmen think he is a man who gives himself airs. Torn and lone, "I am unfit for work — old; I will kill myself." God wants us to be happy, I say. Etcetera. All the boring, felt things one says. Go away from here, I say. Which is saying both too little and too much. I tell him my life, Sheila tells him hers. At sunset I tap her watch—she likes to photograph at this hour; and I do this also in order to release Fiore, because I think he has worn himself out and because I have impertinently said too much. I wonder if he thinks I have dismissed him.

"How small and worn my story sounds," he says. He remembers the word "trite." He kisses our hands, and, proud and sad, crosses the lonely piazza.

I knew this story before I knew this story: the claustrophobia that accompanies the tenderness, the bonds that kill, the loneliness as southern as the love, the loneliness that is accused of superiority, of "putting on airs." I have traveled so far to be back home, bound to the agonizing religion of the family.

To keep people on the farms, the regional government rewards the birth of a boy with seven million lire, the birth of a girl with five hundred thousand lire, and the birth of a calf with three hundred thousand lire. Fiore tells us this.

We are in the clouds, three thousand feet above the sea. There are clouds in my room. There are thirty-six cars in the *piazzetta*, sixteen of them red. The only sound that reaches me unmuffled is that of the bells of the church I face and the answering bells from across the valley, from Caltanissetta. Swallows wheel. ("I don't know how many birds I saw. Were they a definite or indefinite number? This problem involves the question of the existence of God. If God exists, the number is definite, because how many birds I saw is known to God. If God does not exist, the number is indefinite because nobody was able to take count." — Leonardo Sciascia.)

The mists clear, the world is revealed. A crippled woman in royal blue heaves her way up the stairs of the church, three more women in long black dresses and black shawls, a little girl in pink. A butcher stands outside his shop in a white coat. In the air now brittle, sounds waft up, the sandy sound of the street cleaner's broom; and "Onions and potatoes," a peddler calls. A cat snakes down the church steps. There are cutouts — balconies of sorts, protected — in the pitched tile roofs. When the women take the air in them they are not observed from the streets; they sit just as formally as if they were being observed, they sit very still. When the bells ring for eight o'clock Mass I have a chocolate *cornetto*. Chocolate for breakfast in a medieval town.

Dario, the boy-of-all-work at our hotel, implores us over and over again to leave the Audi in the hotel garage, he wants to drive it. He is sixteen. He knew how to drive when he was ten. Why don't you drive? he says to me; all his questions are delivered like utterances, he thinks every question has an answer (which of course it does; but my answers give rise only to more flat questions: Why. Where are you going. *I am going to the cafe*. But why do you want to go there.) He thinks every action has a single motive. He left school because he hated to study and because he made all the teachers angry. He is sweet. In New York City he would be a criminal. Perhaps he is a criminal. He likes to talk about robberies and stolen cars and rapes: "In Catania there are *real* thieves." It is hard to tell whether he is smart or dopey. *How much does your car cost. How does the alarm work. Why don't you have husbands.*

Sheila tells Dario about her husband, Giuseppe, it gives her pleasure to talk of him. I invent a husband, to shut him up; Dario reminds me of my aunts, their implacable question: Why. He cannot understand why two women should be traveling alone, he makes assumptions: *Why do you have single rooms.*

Dario's mother has five children. She must have another, he says. Why? To laugh and play with, he says. Otherwise how will she laugh and play?

It is high summer and we are back in Palermo for the feast of Santa Rosalia, who saved the city from the plague. The streets are dressed in crimson and canary-yellow banners; on the terraces of my hotel oil wicks burn in little terra-cotta dishes. From my balcony I see, through a lacy curtain of pines, a flash of red skirts, white upraised arms, slender graceful hands clapping — I sense as much as see the movements of the dancers *folklorico*. For all its energy and apparent spontaneity, the dance is as rigidly choreographed as it has been for centuries (and as hot). Poignant songs and ribald songs, Arab wails, operatic trills . . . songs about courting and killing, about lovers and sisters and mistresses and mamas, never about wives.

In the Capo, revelers are eating fried sliced spleen on caraway buns.

In another part of town an old man watches fireworks from his balcony above the railroad tracks, eating ices. He doesn't mind the noise of the trains, he says, he has lived here forty-four years; only the sounds of their coupling disturb his sleep.

My sleep is perfumed and undisturbed.

OCEAN, WHO IS THE SOURCE OF ALL.

— HOMER, *THE ILIAD*

THE USE OF THE SEA AND AIR IS COMMON TO ALL; NEITHER CAN A TITLE TO THE OCEAN BELONG TO ANY

PEOPLE OR PRIVATE PERSONS, FORASMUCH AS NEITHER NATURE NOR PUBLIC USE AND CUSTOM PERMIT

ANY POSSESSION THEREOF. — ELIZABETH I

THE AEOLIAN ISLAN

THE OCEAN IS A POWERFUL DRUG. IT SEEMS TO EXTEND LIFE BY EXERCISING THE INTELLIGENCE OUTSIDE

OF THE FACTORS WHICH FORMED IT. . . . THE DRAINING CAN BE EXQUISITE.

— RONALD BLYTHE, *THE VIEW FROM WINTER*

On the ferry from Palermo, flesh:

In the gray dawn a nun in dove-gray garments presses against me with the unselfconsciousness of a vocational celibate; this unselfconsciousness is impossible to distinguish from rapacity. . . . The hydrofoil is crowded, hot, its course through the waters an erratic hybrid's course; a middle-aged woman fans her bewildered old mother, who seems distant from everything and everybody, especially herself. The women are wearing identical dresses. The younger woman — who has the unmistakable sweet, bowed look of someone bearing a sacrificial life with grace — pats her mother, who appears oblivious to touch, pats and pats and exhorts her mother to *look! look!* The old lady gazes straight ahead; occasionally a tremor washes through her body. The daughter's fan blows the smell of sweat toward me; it mingles not unpleasantly with the smell of sea.

Limpido! Chiaro! everyone exclaims as we pull into Marina Corta. Emerald waters, clean, clear, in the port of Lipari, a Mediterranean morning miracle.

I am deranged by island light. I forget my luggage. Two island-brown children fetch my bags from the departing boat, grinning. How they run! They weigh less than the bags do.

In the pool an old man is teaching a young boy with flesh as sweet as flowers to swim. In and out of Moorish arches they swim: a cloistered pool. The old man's flesh hangs loose from his hard muscles. In and out of the arches women with breasts like small round apples swim. Children offer a litter of kittens the gold foil that butter has been wrapped in; we hear the animals' noisy scraping as their rough tongues secure the golden fat.

"Silence and a gulf of air . . ." The young people fled from Lipari, its solitude. "Eat bread and *cipolle* and stay in Lipari" . . . but they ran away; and now Lipari, the largest island of Ulysses' archipelago, all "brine and shine and whirling wind," is fashionable with the children of fashion . . . birds of paradise whose plumage astounds.

Wild geraniums grow alongside the road, above the sea, the beaches, and the coves. Lacy fennel, blue-green, grows among volcanic hills, its soapy perfume mingles with the fresh green, pungent smell of wild mint; and with their bread and onions the people of Lipari eat eggs poached in water to which has been added drops of good oil and small cubes of hard cheese and peeled tomato and wild mint.

Sun-dazed in this gentle place, I dream and wait for sunset, resting against dry walls that surround a house that has been here for four hundred years; the house is covered with vines, it is asleep.

Two women, one astride a donkey carrying kindling, pass by. They wear flowered babushkas as protective as monks' cowls. Their gaze glances off us, we are people who come and go, people of no consequence to the island to which they are bound. Their weathered faces are maps of dumb endurance; their eyes have seen the world.

I ask my driver whether there are drugs here, Mafiosi. "I am Italian," he says, glaring, "not Sicilian." Then he gives me a wild anemone, a lily of the field.

How hospitably these green hills meet the sea. Even the rocks here seem domestically inclined.

"The indulgence with which we now treat our young children produces all the tenderness of our modern natures."
— *Giambattista Vico*

On balconies the women sit with backs to the street and to the sea, faces toward familiar home.

In the beauty parlor, Nuccio, who cuts my hair, says blondes have "dead bones," whereas a woman *oscura* is "vivace."

I read in a magazine that Sophia Loren regards her image in the beauty-parlor mirror for hours, as if it were a painting; but all Italian women do this . . . and smile and smile and smile.

In an antique shop I see a nativity in a bell jar.

There are two bays in the town of Lipari, two ports, one for ferries, one for hydrofoils and yachts. The long narrow spiffy Corso connects them, a satisfying state of affairs.

Above the modern town are the Castello and the Acropolis, surrounded by stone walls — high; and succinctly in the middle of things. The history of Lipari from neolithic times is in this enclosure. There is the cathedral, domed, baroque, and there are six other churches, small (seven is a pleasing number). There is the Archeological Museum: 147 amphorae harvested from wild seas, arranged all close and lavishly in steps, their sandy scaliness suggesting depths of obsidian black and old rose; barbaric jewelry; glazed pots and masks; sarcophagi. A tangible history lesson among oleanders and cicadas.

The museum shop sells pink booties.

The tunneled entrance to the Spanish fort is cool and dark and smells acrid and sweet: mildew and roses.

On tombs set among ancient pines children sit and drink bittersweet Chinotto. They prefer sitting on tombs — and so do lovers, entwined — to sitting formally in the new stone amphitheater, which, deceptively Greek, commands a view of the moody sea . . . and is the arena for *Harry Loves Sally* and *Born on the Fourth of July*.

The sea is moody. Boats cut turquoise swaths through broody flint-dark waters. Horns and seagulls. The essential business of the sea: the sound — clean, quick, clear, snappy — of a lipstick-red tanker dropping anchor. The skies are purple-thunder-clouded; but it doesn't rain. It almost never rains in these islands (and when it does the rain is soft, and caught by cisterns), where pleasures are these: the deliciousness of fresh water after salt water on one's sun-loved body; the white-blue-yellow, infinite, cordial air. The path to a grand hotel: down a winding lane past winding stone walls, through tunnels of bougainvillea. The intimate lap of water on rock; the consternation a sparrow makes on an oleander branch. Bicycles built for four. "The uncreated light."

Flesh is the bower of bone.

Interior lives: a fat woman braids the hair of a child. They live in one room: a stove, a sink, a bed, a table. The room is open the the street. The one-room house is a hundred years old. Its door is garlanded with peppers and tomatoes and onions and sprays of oregano from the shop next door. From the depths and shadows of the room emerges an old lady in black, carrying her knitting.

On the beach at the Marina Lunga there are hotels, some are dignified, some are hovels ("Showers for Sale"). Tonight there is a *festa*: beach towels with dirty pictures, caramelized peanuts, garden furniture, posters of Marilyn Monroe, dresses, calzone, plastic toys. Italian-looking dogs. A crazy lady with army boots and tube socks and a lace-curtain skirt; a shoeless man selling balloons; a pop singer in clogs; a two-year-old with crocheted socks and patent leather shoes. I am the only tourist here. Are people the same all over the world? I nip into church. (Every port has a church.) Outside, the loudspeakers are blaring: Stevie Wonder and Paul

LIPARI.

McCartney singing *Ebony and Ivory.* My mind, in
overdrive, races. I think: Fellini. I think: Andy
Hardy. How can both be true? Both can be true. A
coincidence of opposites. People are the same, they
aren't the same; there are textural differences
(within contextual differences) that register only
subliminally; they excite and disturb the mind.

This is not Coney Island.

I want to stay here all night.

The silky air is crisped by sea breezes. Crown
of thorns: on a balcony crowded with pots of the
prickly plant precariously poised, a woman with
long streaked blond hair stands, her daughter clinging to her skirts. They are watching the ferries. The
ferries are named after artists: Filippo Lippi, Giovanni Bellini, Donatello, Piero della Francesca.
Perhaps I am attributing my own sadness to the
woman; but I know: for her, now, the ships will
always be going out, each departure is one more
departure in an endless series of departures.

At a harbor cafe two men play guitars and sing
about lost loves. They sing to each other because
there are no women to sing to here. I long to join
them, and I go home.

Bodies float on water, voices float on air.

At Campo Bianco there is a mountain of white
pumice. Abandoned loading jetties stretch into the
sea. Young men slide from the top of the pumice
mountain into the sea. They climb like Sisyphus;
they fall — leaping, sliding, slipping — like Icarus;
they climb again. They leave white clouds from the
pumice in the blue waters, we swim in milk. The
pumice mountain is "like face powder," someone
says; "like an old man's dream of powdered snow,
warm and soft," Sheila says. In the blue and violet
waters it feels, underfoot, like the undulating skin of
a snake.

The Agnelli yacht, awaiting its owner, is covered with decorative white awnings, swathed in an
Arabian-tentlike cocoon, its mahogany sheathed in

THE AIO.

*"No one who has never seen himself surrounded on
all sides by nothing but the sea can have a true
conception of the world and of his own relation to it."*
— *Goethe*, Italian Journey

white bunting. Like a girl in curlers on Saturday night. Next to it is a yacht from one of the Arab emirates, stark white and shuttered, its windows silvered like mirrors and black. It looks like a hospital ship—only one can't imagine it on a mission of mercy; it looks like a ship designed for quarantine.

I am on a yacht, too, the *Aio*, the Sardinian word for *andiamo*; for ten days I will be living a water life . . .

Water has skin. The waters slip over one another like the notes of a Mozart quintet. They shine electrically as if they were illuminated from the core of the world. . . .

Why is doing nothing on a boat not doing nothing? Because one is in a state of active trust. I have surrendered to the winds, the currents, and the sun, I am at their disposal. "To surrender" is an active verb. I am entertaining the wind and the sun, my body is the host. The coconut matting on the deck is smooth under my back. From where I lie, neither asleep nor awake, I have a foreshortened view, I see the calves and the feet and the flapping sandals of the crew: Sunday, who is from Nigeria, and John, who is from Nigeria, too, Paulo, and Alvaro, the handsome young Florentine captain (one earring and a beard), and Big Dorothy, the cook, born in Poland, raised in Israel, married to Rome. Paulo's legs are covered with wiry red hair . . . Black legs and white legs and red legs. . . . Crayola has stopped production of some of its colors, news that didn't trouble me at the time I heard it. Like the addition of two states to the Union and several hundred new FM stations, it signaled my getting older in a constantly new if not refreshed world. Here the world is constantly refreshed. I fall asleep and dream Crayola dreams and I wake to the innumerable blues of the water world. I want all the colors of the world and I want them never to fade. "Motion fans fresh our wits with wonder."

Dorothy likes to discourse on the iconography of paintings, Donald Trump, Nouveau and deco architecture, medieval armor, Mayan history, and the virtues of American apple pie; she was once a sergeant in the Israeli army, now she lives in a shipyard in Rome, surrounded by cats. These are the luncheons she prepares: zucchini frittata with mixed green salad, white peaches, and Pino Grigio. Ricotta insalata; Pecorino; tiny tomatoes dressed in olive oil; small pears and white figs equal in size; Malvasia, dessert wine from the island of Salina. Eggplant mousse, white and creamy; beef *stracciato* over rice and mounds of fresh green beans; lemon cake made with lemons from Sorrento and *limoncello* — homemade lemon liqueur from Sorrento, which smells like all the citrus gardens in the world and is very, very strong. (The eggplant mousse is "stupidly simple," she says. "You place the eggplant directly on the flame and then you clean the stove all day." But it isn't she who cleans.) Pasta with *ceci* (which the Neapolitans call "thunder and lightning"). Pasta with a puree of peppers and tomatoes and cream; turkey breast with sage, parsley, butter, oil; shredded carrots in lemon. Pasta with roe of sea bass and olive oil. Baby octopus marinated in lemon; they are lovely, they are the same color as pink hibiscus, and just as fleshy. D. H. Lawrence called them "ink-pots" — Michelangelo drew with the ink of squid — and pronounced them "the consistency of boiled cellulid, . . . tougher than indiarubber, gristly through and through"; he says that female polyps are caught and used to snare and catch male polyps; but I have never seen this. One day begins with a long breakfast discussion of the evening's *panzanella* — a fisherman's stew of tomatoes, anchovies, tuna — whatever comes to hand; there is a solemn discussion of the bread for the stew — how old it must be, how much there must be, how long it must be soaked — and onions, to use or not to use?

The simplicity of Italian food requires patience and perfection of execution.

A hundred years ago Vulcano erupted. Entirely volcanic (the island where blacksmith Vulcan made lightning for Jupiter), its colors — vermilion, bitter yellow, moss green, purple, blue (the work of sulfur, alum, and ferrous oxides) — intensify after noon. The island resort smells of rotten eggs.

Sulfurous, burning volcanic mud pours into a natural basin of earth, forming a stinking pool said to be efficacious for neuralgia, phlebitis, and skin diseases, "nasal complaints," and diseases of the "female genital apparatus," rheumatism and respiratory problems. Gas bubbles rise to the surface of the hot pot, from which one can emerge clean (though stinking), unless one chooses to reach down to the slippery floor of the pool and anoint oneself with the stuff.

Young people do it for fun. The girl lovingly anointing her nipples does not have rheumatism in mind.

The repulsive smell of sulfur insinuates itself into restaurants and the orchid-festooned courtyards of boutiques, and shelters in the pores of bathers.

The pool looks like a pot of bubbling gray gravy.

The gray mud turns blank white on exposed bodies; Gianni and Umberto meet us on the tar road covered like savages with dead clay; they perform a self-parody. "Have you ever made eet weeth a satyr?"

A naked man with wire glasses, entirely self-absorbed, sits Buddha-style in the pool, his knobby knees protruding from the water; the muddy hair on his chest looks like hoar frost. An old man and his old wife sit up to their necks in mud, impassively side by side, looking straight ahead . . . this is how they have gone through life, side by side, not touch-

VULCANO.

"A crystal, a flower or a shell stands out from the usual disorder that characterizes most perceptible things. They are privileged forms that are more intelligible for the eye, even though more mysterious for the mind, than all the others we see indistinctly."
— Paul Valéry,
"Les Merveilles de la Mer," in Les Coquillages.
Collection Isis.

ing. Pink porcine heads rising from gray mud. Heads on clay platters. An old man in a striped silk dressing gown, a young woman in a bikini bottom.

On shelves and in ovenlike openings in the rocks surrounding the pool, bodies place themselves, jealously guarding their chosen spots, to bathe in steam and gases that issue forth in geysers and puffs. Fango-painted faces, eyes peering out of mud masks: they look like the faces of deranged raccoons. Pilgrims climb the serrated rock to the Great Crater to lose themselves in clouds of steam; they look like zombies, adherents of a primeval, savage rite.

THIS TOO GOD HAS CREATED FOR OUR BLESS-ING reads a sign near the hot pot. But gum sandals, floats, orange balls, a bright green Vespa, everything in the vicinity of the pool, assumes a fetishistic look.

The clear water of the nearby beach is a natural Jacuzzi. I step on soggy cigarette butts on my way to the burning water; I burn my ankles and turn back. YOU CANNOT KNOW HOW EFFICACIOUS THESE WATERS ARE UNTIL YOU IMMERSE YOUR SOUL AND REST IN THE HAND OF GOD . . . THIS CALDRON OF TRANSFORMING MUSIC AND COLORS. I do not know whether this sign is an endorsement or a disclaimer. My flesh has turned raw pink.

Sheila and Umberto and Franca and Gianni and Bruno climb three winding kilometers on slippery soil and vertical rocks to the Great Crater — Bruno stamps the bushes for snakes; "You get there and there is a big hole," Umberto says. But Sheila says it is a wonder of the world — pale yellow and brilliant yellow crystallized rock and sulfuric smoke. They all burn their ankles. Their throats ache from the corrosive fumes. I sit, instead, in a bar with Dorothy, who shops for provisions in a white Victorian underdress. I have a ricotta *cornetto*, Dorothy has a peach *granita* with cream and a brioche; she dips into the creamy peach with the brioche as one

would dunk into coffee with a doughnut; children all do this too, very intently. When there is so little to do, everything there is to do becomes a ritual.

We shunt back and forth between the islands, weaving in and out of grottoes, coves, *faraglioni* — tall standing rocks in the middle of the sea, one with a square door cut in it, and one absurdly like the profile of a Roman soldier with a helmet on. From the sea the Great Crater is a pink cone with fingers of gray running down its sides like icing on a cake. The houses of Vulcano are white, the doors and windows are outlined in soft pastels; their economical owners reach from the window and paint with color as far as the brush can reach and no farther.

We swim from a black sand beach flecked with the red of iron. I can see to the bottom of the ocean — 30 meters; I see a lobster pot, bright red. In this sifted light, in this live air, every color glows, "each shape and shadow shows." I assume a position of complete passivity, and Sheila and Umberto tow me in, each holding a hand as I float, 150 meters from the beach to the boat.

But one day I abandon trust, or faith abandons me. In the deep water Gianni and Umberto make a cradle seat for me with their crossed arms to heave me into the orange Zodiac, the little rubber dinghy that will return us to the yacht. I don't trust the buoyancy of the water; I doubt their strength is equal to the task of lifting and hoisting me over the dauntingly rounded sides of the Zodiac, on which I can get no purchase. I have misgivings about the size of my body. I can't relax and trust it to their care. I panic. Umberto keeps saying that he needs to prove himself, although what he has to prove I cannot imagine, because surely the failure to be lifted is mine. Men are strange. As a consequence of failure he drives the Zodiac, with me in it, dangerously fast, one hundred miles an hour, to the yacht; I could have predicted this. Men can't help themselves.

"This morning I shall tell the simple happiness of a man stretched out in the hollow of a boat. The oblong shell of a skiff has closed over him. He is sleeping. An almond. The boat, like a bed, espouses sleep."
— *Gaston Puel*, Le chant entre deux astres

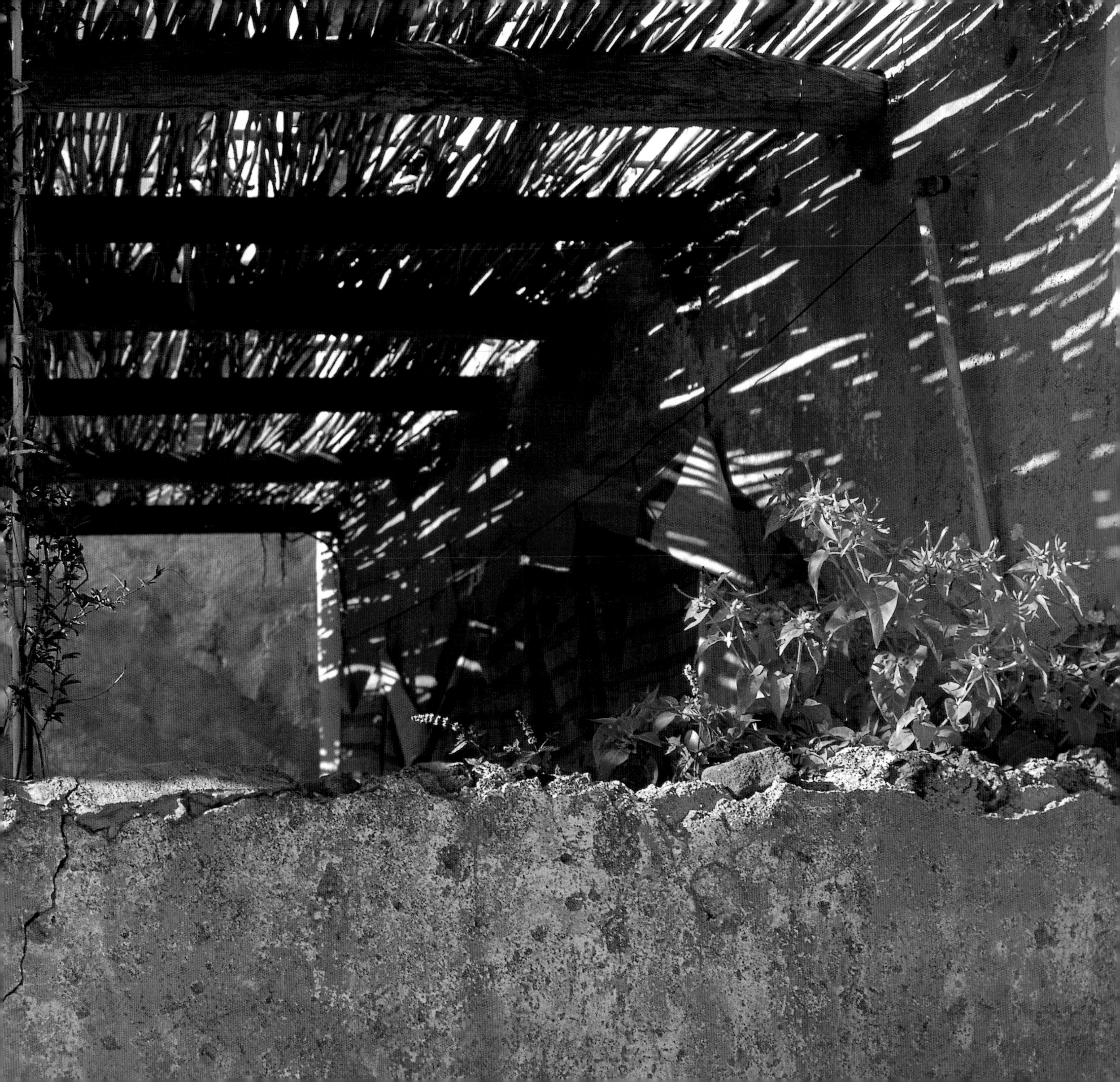

My father once told me a story, a folk tale, about why the sea is salt; it weighs on my mind that I have forgotten it.

It is impossible, where Bruno and Gianni, father and son, are concerned, to tell where love leaves off and competition begins. They climb the pumice mountain and slip and slide and fall together. In India a man needs a son to bury him. In Italy a man needs a son in order to have a worthy opponent. Gianni and Bruno throw pumice rocks at each other; they are always taking each other by surprise.

We sail through glass-blue days.

We are docked off Lipari. An oompah band breaks the morning peace. From the yacht we see the band marching down the long road to the long black beach: blue caps and buttoned white shirts, two by two and smiling; the assertive oompah sound mingles happily with the slap and hum of outboard motorboats and horns and the high sweet singing of nuns: *Ave Maria.* Our Lady is being asked to protect the harbor. Bells carillon wildly and the noise of cannons thunders off velvet hills.

Where is the procession? Umberto asks. He can't see the procession because he is in the middle of it; there is a metaphor in this. We are one of many boats, large and small, rough and elegant, all flower-bedecked; waterborne priests in bright vestments intone the Glorious Mysteries and in their midst blue-and-silver-cloaked *carabinieri* stand proud and erect and Coast Guardsmen tenderly guard improvised wooden crosses . . . whistles; and *Salve!* most ancient, friendly greeting . . . *Now and in the hour of our death* . . . Mary is escorted

with flowers. Fireworks surround the most pacific of women (and the strongest). "Wild air, world-mothering air / nestling me everywhere" . . . Oh, if death were such a sailing!

Dorothy, having had a row with Sunday, is in the galley listening to *Carmina Burana.*

In the morning a khaki-and-red helicopter whirls over the hills. Two *carabinieri* on motorcycles and two in a car race up and down the beach road, a third of a kilometer. We think that this noisy extended foreplay means Agnelli is coming at last. Umberto gets the scoop: the cycles and the car and the (Keystone) cops are all in aid of a thirteen-year-old boy on a Vespa. In Italy (where there is a law for everything and the law exists to be broken) there are regulations governing the speed of a Vespa; the speed depends upon a complicated ratio of horsepower and age of driver and age of Vespa . . . Umberto laughs so hard he cannot finish his story.

The better part of one evening is spent discussing the relative merits of Malvasia and *limoncello:* Is Malvasia *meno o più forte, meno o più dolce? meno forte e più dolce? meno o più aromatica? più gialla o meno?* This conversation inspires a conversation about coffee bars and coffee: *chiaro, o scuro, corretto, macchiato, lungo, doppio con latte, latte a parte, con schiuma, senza schiuma* . . . and on and on and on.

Swept away . . .

I am the only American on the yacht. "Italians are all manners and graces," a visitor says; "by this time Americans would be asking one another how they *felt* and *why* they felt as they did . . . or why they *thought* they felt as they did . . ."

Umberto tells us about friends in Trapani whose doors are unlocked all summer long, members of the extended family come and go without notice or warning, "it is really all one big kitchen," he says, and they bring their cars and their caravans. I feel lonely. I miss my brother, his oily smelly little fishing boat on Staten Island. Neither this vessel nor his suits me exactly. Classlessness is not necessarily liberating.

In our shipshape streamlined world of teak and sails and privilege there is often talk of the regrettable pleasure palaces of "the masses," the new housing developments that are beginning to burgeon in the archipelago. Every time I hear someone — from the Left or from the Right — speak of "the masses" I grind my teeth. What abstractions are these? (My paternal grandfather was a shepherd; my maternal grandfather was a carpenter . . .)

Sometimes at night there are shaded references to past infidelities . . .

I smell John's spicy deodorant when he serves meals. One day he is asked to bring some figs from the galley; panic is written on his face. His overeagerness to please interferes with his comprehension. It is clear that he will go to the galley and pray that "feegs" — whatever they may be — will declare themselves and jump off the shelves for him. He returns with a box of cookies. "When you don't understand me," Umberto says, "you must say, 'Master, I don't understand.' Is that clear, John?" Oh yes, clear. "English is the language you speak to servants in," Franca says. My stomach lurches twice over. All else aside, I feel like a paying guest in an English spinster's novel. . . .

The avid desire to know and to be known, the eagerness, seems fabulously American to me now. . . .

Sometimes my host flirts routinely, in an enervated way, as if an American would be disappointed if he were not to make meaningless passes. I hate this and I say so, which he regards as a breach of contract. . . .

The sun sets behind sturdy *faraglioni*. Umberto and Gianni sing Sard songs, the lights of the houses on shore twinkle.

We wake to a white morning, a bleached day. The rock lava monsters of Vulcano make lewd, impertinent gestures.

Bruno returns from fishing holding aloft strange fan-shaped encrusted mollusks with stony spines, orange, red, gray. They are about two feet long, they have beards, and they taper to a kind of silver beak. Sunday says they are full of meat and good to eat. Dorothy says they are not. Sheila says their eyes are open, but I can't see their eyes, only Sheila can see their eyes. Franca says the freak things are oysters and looks for the pearl in them. John says mushrooms grow from them. Umberto says they are sea scallops. Gianni says they are fossils. Sheila says, How can they be, if they have eyes? It is finally settled that they are giant mussels; inside one of them is a baby lobster.

Umberto caught an octopus but it caught him too and then before he was able to kill it with a dart gun it escaped.

Gianni cannot take a woman's hand without kissing it.

Rosella, pretty as a princess, lives in an eighteenth-century house in the middle of Sorrento; when you enter the garden, she says, shut away from the noisy tourists is a paradise of lemon trees and orange trees. She lives in this house with her grandmother, they share a bedroom. She has brought oranges with her. At sunset we all eat Sorrentine oranges, the delicious sticky liquid running down our chins and mingling with the salty sweat of our bodies. Then we swim.

Salina is the greenest island, an ardent impressionist dream of wild geraniums, high corn, hollyhocks, cactus, prickly pears, chestnut trees, eucalyptus, ferns, magnolias. Its two mountain ridges — extinct volcanoes — slip into the sea like exhausted breasts. It looks as I imagine Hawaii might look if Hawaii had a population of two thousand souls.

Walls of black, white, and gray tufa fretted and carved by winds line the way to the mountaintops. Salina is chaste (it makes that beautiful strumpet Capri look decadent) and inviting, and now the beautiful young people are beginning to come, and the road has come, and Salina's sweet majestic simplicity is yielding to the demand for tourist amenities. The young people of the island left years ago.

In church I count sixteen simpering Marys under bell jars. A livid open-mouthed Jesus, his teeth bared in a rictus grin, refutes the victory of the Resurrection. A very old lady — so old she looks almost like an infant; so old, so young, in such a little space — tells me that God is in a cupboard and asks me where everybody has gone. *Why have they left*, she cries.

There is something witchy about this place. I have been here before. I have not been here before. But I know this house: hot pink flattered by purple bougainvillea, its striped green-and-white umbrella, the vermilion water tap, the green cubes of windows and doors, the grapevines that fall with artful negligence around them . . . of course. Before the coming of the road the young people left to live in Libya, in Tripoli and Benghazi. I have lived in Libya. I have lived in this house. . . . I eat a strawberry ice.

Gianni says Salina is *triste*. The moment he says this it becomes true.

Panarea is the "floating islet" of the Odyssey. When the sun is hot and the sea is calm, it floats above itself, a doppelganger dream.

The simple cubes of fishermen's houses are now elaborated upon, verandaed and glossed; beautiful brats sit in the harbor bar with their exotic dogs, wearing sneakers and net, satin and straw and skintight jersey, with the appearance of artlessness, smoking and eating ices. (They wear jewels and indecipherable T-shirts: AMERICANNINO, 218 TRUONG-TAN-BUI STREET SAIGON (VERY CLOSE TO TAN-SON-NHU AIRPORT); THE SECRET LIFE OF JP.) Of course, having made the island into an oasis of privilege, they are determined to preserve its rusticity. There are no street lights on Panarea (houses and shops are lit with lanterns, an elegant way to create magic) and no cars; three-wheeled *api* — so named because the open vehicles make a noise

PANAREA.

Who will tell the story of rocks? To sail around these islands is to see a story unfold; but the story is in a language I don't know.

About mountains it is true that chance left free to act falls into an order as well as a purpose.

We cut through the sea as if it were butter. There are storm systems all over the Adriatic; Stromboli smolders in a milky blue haze. The white of the sky is unwholesome: layers of gauze drawn over lead. Anonymous voices on the ship's radio — *Olio-Olie* — sound like lost children at dusk, waiting to be called home. Stromboli rumbles. I smell the fountains of smoke that are received by fountains of smoke on the summit of the northeast crater. The rumbles are hard to distinguish from the sound of waves. *Si lamenta*, the Italians say: it is groaning, it it laments. The beaches here are an uncompromising black; the water is black, and then an arbitrary greenness begins. Rock particles as fine as mist slip down the face of the mountain after the lament ends. The others swim, I don't. I am experiencing a surfeit of sensation. You must take some risks, Umberto tells me, which excites my anger. I eat a greengage plum and watch its yellow pulp plummet to the ocean floor.

On an otherwise deserted mountain face, on the extreme edge of vulnerability, are three white houses in a clannish clutch; and fruit trees and grapevines. A man hang-glides off the mountain. I see him, but I don't believe in him; he is a dream. It

is absurd and absurdly touching to see gay *ombrellini* on the black beaches of a volcano that is in constant eruption, constantly re-creating itself, it is brave. Creation itself never ceases, but one labors in the dark to understand one's part in it.

After he swims, Umberto says, It really wasn't safe to swim there. I like him for this.

John smiles only in the water; he closes his eyes and smiles. John and Sunday and Dorothy and Alvaro shampoo their hair in the water and then they play catch with the shampoo bottle. A shoal of flying fish inquires into their play.

From the yacht the whiteness of the village repels, it is a blankness as obscure as darkness. But in its embrace one is enchanted. A steep flight of steps is occasionally transected at right angles by streets of tiles, culs-de-sacs that lead to white houses, groomed gardens, riotous courtyards. (Here is a house: white; lemon-yellow shutters; white undershirts flapping on the line; a blue Vespa parked under lemon trees and magnolias.) The steps, which form the main street of the village, lead to a bifurcated road; each fork (there is no necessity in such a place to grieve for the road not taken) takes one past rounded corners of souklike white buildings and under Moorish arches and past intimate ruined farms. It is cool; the trees are burdened late in their year with lemons and with figs, unripe.

A strange fruit grows here, we had it in our garden in Tripoli; it is neither a lemon nor a grapefruit, it is swollen and misshapen and it has grotesque carbuncular protuberances — it is a malignant fruit. It is strange what can grow in one's garden without occasioning wonder. Only in memory do I think: Such strange fruit; in Tripoli I never gave it a

thought, perhaps because I was unhappy, and it was rooted in my garden.

The forks of the road meet at a belvedere where there is an ugly church, and on this belvedere there is a coffee bar called the Ingrid Club. The house where Ingrid Bergman lived when she worked with Rossellini on *Stromboli* is painted lipstick red.

This is the most romantic island. The light is honey sweet, lambent, pellucid, born of water and fire. Everything it touches is graced, everything is classically clear but softly harmonized.

Black night and a marvel of stars, "vaulty, voluminous, stupendous." Sea and sky and stars and air combine into one element; this is another kind of air, a new sky. Stromboli is showering arcs and arrows of pure red fire into the sky. The fire gushes up and then slides down its ordained infernal path till, with the clink and splash of rock, it reaches the water. It reaches the beach where Umberto swam this morning: fire, rock, water, one element. I am chastened by the spectacle. My companions' faces glow in the light of the fire, which takes their words away (*Oooooh*). It is not possible to maintain a social manner in the face of such a phenomenon. For these moments we are all united. An inky blot of smoke holds up the stars.

"From such an ocean must have come the horses of Rhesus, which were made pregnant by Zephyr, the west wind of Greece; and on the shores of the same Ocean the horse of Achilles, also begotten by Zephyr, must have been born. Later the geographers, observing that the whole earth, like a great island, was girt by the sea, called Ocean all the waters by which the land is surrounded."
— *Giambattista Vico*

STROMBOLI AND ETNA
IN THE DISTANCE.

From the sea the thousands and thousands of cactus plants on terraced Alicudi seem like cut velvet, soft.

Alicudi is the least self-conscious of the islands, it doesn't even have a disco. Boats (Trasporti Alimentari) bring in produce and water. All the roads are streets of stairs. It is a casbah, a maze of alleys. There is one car in the port. It is wrapped in cellophane like hard candy. It is red. It was won in a lottery, but it is useless except as an icon.

From behind a buff-colored house emerges a platinum blonde, tall and beautiful in a black bikini, a Gucci bag slung over her shoulder. Two gnarled and thick ancient olive trees stand at the entrance to a narrow alley; a slender nun in white stands between them.

There is a grotto so big near the island of Filicudi — La Grotta del Bue Marino — that a tourist ferry can enter it. It was thought in ancient times to be the home of a sea monster; but perhaps this was a fear of birth, or of woman, for its waters are warm and gentle like the waters of the womb, our first cave-home. Our orange Zodiac enters the luminescent blue waters and I swim, I float: a fugue state; born again in water: "What would the world be, once bereft / of wet and of wilderness? Let that be left, O let them be left, wilderness and wet."

The terraces and dry walls of little Filicudi, the stingy roads that lead to isolated communities, were built before World War II for an agricultural people whose crops were grain and olives and wine. In 1955 there was an exodus; there were two thousand people on Filicudi then; there are two hundred people on Filicudi now.

I felt bleak when I first saw Filicudi — imagine living in a stone cube that sprouts from stone with the meager color and comfort of prickly pears around one; what is it to live here? Imagine a stone house, windows and doors whitewashed, alone on a rocky beach; what is a life here? Then I met Stefano, all the colors of his life.

Stefano has a long gray beard and is grizzled and wears safari clothes and drives a Willys American jeep left over from the war, when the roads were good — they are not good now. He is the island's unofficial public relations man (the population of Filicudi swells to two thousand in the summer). "Of all the houses on the island, mine is the most beautiful," he says. His house is on a belvedere overlooking a long black sandy beach, the sea. In his garden grow hibiscus and pigeons, bougainvillea, chickens and basil bushes and figs, tomatoes, onions — that sweet disorder that looks ordained to be. It is a friendly one-room house: stove, hearth, TV, long rough kitchen table, sturdy chairs, beds discreetly placed. There is a well, a mule. The house recognizes no distinction between outside and in, it is an all-weather, welcoming house. Stefano's sister is visiting his ancient mother (eighty-seven), she is irritable and comes from Milan.

Stefano's mother worked "on Seventh Avenue" for seven years, from 1942 to 1949. I understand her Italian more perfectly than I understand the cultivated Italian spoken on the yacht. We respond to each other with a sympathy that is physical and immediate, she kisses me with her dry old lips and her kiss is sweet. She is perfectly groomed. She recites, for our mutual pleasure, place names in New York: Fourth Place, Brooklyn; Hell's Kitchen; Second Avenue . . . The names go on and on. I haven't been so happy since the trip began. Her irritable daughter longs for us to go. I think she is hiding a retarded child in the house, from which come sounds of guttural whimpering. . . . How nice it must be to live in a place where everyone says *Salve!* to one another and waves a friendly hand. . . . Stefano's mama offers her frail body, so tenacious of life, for a good-night hug (she is my past, my good grandma, my fairy godmother; and she is my future, too: my age approaching). Disregarding her impatient daughter, Stefano's mother grabs my head between her scratchy hands and whispers — in English — *I am American, too.* I do not know what this means, but I know it is an offering, a confession and a gift.

Stefano drives us to the boat. Tomorrow our water life will be over. "Our evening is over us; our night whelms, whelms, and will end us."

"Don't you agree that life is becoming more superficial?"

"Not everywhere." — Leonardo Sciascia, *The Wine-Dark Sea*

S A R D I N I A

Corrumpere et currumpi seculum vocatur — They call it the spirit of the age

to seduce and be seduced — or, as we would now say, the fashion.

— *The New Science of Giambattista Vico*

PORTO ROTONDO.

The Alisarda flight from Rome to Olbia lasts only thirty-five minutes. I think they must pipe Shalimar through the air vents. I know I've never seen so many Gucci and Vuitton bags in so short a space of time and in one place, and never so much gold lamé in the daytime, nor so many "Filipina" nannies; even the little girls wear bows of gold lamé, impoverishing their look of energetic innocence. I am entering the civilization of idleness.

Sardinia (Sardegna) is the largest island in the Mediterranean, and very old, older geologically than Italy or Sicily; it is to a tiny corner of land in the northeast that the *mondani* — the rich and the beautiful and the worldly — come. They come to a coastal strip of promontories, headlands, bays, inlets, and miraculously clear, striated waters, a new kingdom of hedonism, a yachtsman's paradise among a scented tangle of shrubs and posturing rocks and boulders. If Hawaii smells like sex, the Costa Smeralda smells like money.

A consortium headed by the Aga Khan founded this development in 1962; so desolate and backward was it at the time the Aga Khan saw its playland possibilities that when he offered a fisherman one *miliarde* (one billion lire) for a large parcel of land, the poor fellow, either unable to trust his ears or his good fortune or unable to count so high, said, "No, no, I must have one *milione* [one million], and I want my son to be the *portiere* of the hotel, too." Well, that's how the story goes — lots of stories about the dopey and/or rascally Sards are told by those who have benefited from their terror and revulsion of the sea; it is also said that traditionally the Sards regarded the rocky coast as unlovely and unprofitable, so coastal lands were inherited by daughters, inland plateaus by sons . . . in which case the daughters, and Eleonora d'Arborea, the fourteenth-century queen-judge of Sardinia, her Joan of Arc, have had the last ghostly laugh.

I stay in a settlement, a "village" (villas for rent, villas for sale) just outside of Porto Rotondo, which, strictly speaking, is not part of the Costa Smeralda (it lies south of the Aga Khan's earliest development, and the consortium does not govern its planning and development); but this is a distinction without a difference. No one would pay these prices to be anywhere *but* the Costa Smeralda . . .

I have been in beautiful places before. It's the aggressive prettiness of this place — to say nothing of its pricyness, fifteen dollars for a long drink — that I find stunning. A little bit of Old Mexico on Italian soil. Also Santa Fe. Also Disneyland, also Key West. An approximation of folk art: Med/mod. An army of gardeners nurturing star jasmine, bougainvillea, homely zinnias, malicious-looking lantana, hibiscus, morning glories, alien petunias. Hedges of rosemary (which in fairy tales is watered with milk and will not grow in the gardens of the wicked). The villas — native stone, wood, plaster — differ slightly from one another and follow the rolling contours of the land; and from patios the view is of the saving sea. Could I, if I had planned this community, done it better? I don't see how. So why am I cranky? Why do I feel like that fellow in *The Prisoner*, straining for freedom from a place that has no walls? I am always getting lost.

"Tell him I'm at Andrea Benetton's," a voice sings out.

"Tell him I'm at Krizia's," sounds another.

"No girls," a young friend reports glumly, his evening's exertions having yielded no harvest. "You need a yacht to pick up a girl here." He has only a motorcycle, a Red Rose.

Why should I be so churlish as to quarrel with perfection? Because this place is too rich for me to mainline into my imagination; and I look for the worm in the apple. Or, as the owner of a pub in Porto Rotondo says, this settlement is "troppa fan-

PUNTA VOLPE.

"The earth is full of thy riches. So is this great and
wide sea, wherein are things creeping
innumerable, both small and great beasts. There go
the ships: there is that leviathan, whom thou hast
made to play therein. These wait all upon thee."
— Psalm 104

tasia," a Marie Antoinette-ish conceit of perfection, the upper classes living in houses made to resemble those of shepherds (and dumping their garbage in circular stone constructions made to look like Phoenician dwellings), the dry walls mimicking the walls-without-mortar of the interior, those incoherently meandering walls with their little footpaths where shepherds walk. And whispering of adulteries in the bar in the square . . .

But such a pretty square, with its converging Piranesi-like lines, such a charming *piazzetta*, the happy children happily contained in it so safe in their play. (One always thinks, with Italian children, that one can see the shape of things to come; they claim their looks, their style, their beauty, so young.) And here is Dune, the nine-year-old daughter of the bar's friendly manager, she sings a song to me (these are the only words she knows in English): *I love my little house | Its windows and its doors | Two chimneys on the roof | And a patch of grass before*. "What means weendows?" Dune asks. She hugs me and an albino puppy with equal fervor.

Across the bay the mountains slink like lemurs. The boulders prickle like aroused porcupines.

From two to four in the afternoon, children are forbidden to swim in the pool, it is the time when all good people eat and rest. Very civilized, I call it . . . and I break the rule; Dune and I play in the pool overlooking the sea, the boats. A man and a woman kiss on the myrtle-lined path to the beach (a beach of many coves and hideaway places: yellow umbrellas, and orderly ladders descending to the pacific sea here, vertiginous plunges to frothy waves there; tame and wild, married). They make their way to the pool and enter it, kissing open-mouthed. They are eating each other up alive, waltzing breast to breast in the warm waters of the pool. Dune shouts: I LOVE MY LITTLE HOUSE!

PORTO CERVO.

Dinner on the patio. People here speak in very low voices; this is high-density living. (Italians never seem to mind being in proximity to one another; why should they?) These buildings look like large villas, but in fact they are literally stacked on top of one another and next to one another. It occurs to me that I am living in a very expensive rabbit hutch.

I eat a perfect melon.

I don't like planned communities. I want a Renaissance villa or a bungalow in the Catskills. I do like planned communities, provided they are medieval or Renaissance: Pienza; Siena.

At five o'clock I wake; and I realize that those voices, so hushed, have crowded out and replaced the breathing of the sea, which speaks to me now. There are two nice brown legs emerging from a long white Victorian nightgown; they are mine. There are white bougainvillea blossoms on the terra-cotta floor. White clouds scud across an enamel-blue sky. I wait for the indiscriminately blessing light.

I walk to the beach. Wild frangipani lines the path. Turquoise and jade and emerald and sapphire waters are crystal in my cupped hands. Sun-browned children lean against pines and eat yogurt and read comic books. Outside the mouth of the protected cove, the waves beat. The water is perfect. One makes one's way to it across slimy pebbles, sharp rocks. Old women and young women and men of astounding beauty carefully pick their way across the pebbles and the rocks, like figures in an allegory. Rocks masquerade as seaweed, seaweed as rocks; nothing — a small silver fish slips between my fingers — is what it seems. I am in turquoise water. I move toward sapphire waters, but they elude me. The closer I get, the farther they recede; this is a trip into another country and I cannot find the border; where I am it is always turquoise no matter where I am.

Time is circular and continuous here.

A young man teaches a little boy to swim. His tenderness is exquisite and well rewarded; no gesture he makes is gratuitous or insincere.

I am leaning against a sun-warmed rock. The difference between rocks and human beings, Teilhard said, is that human beings yearn. These rocks yearn.

How can light so soft define so sharply?

Italians do not observe rules. One rule they consistently observe: DO NOT GO IN THE WATER WITHOUT SHOWERING, the signs near the pool say. This they do. They shower to go into the ocean.

On the barbecue where we grill our perfect chicken there are signs saying Don't do this, Don't do that . . . only in Italian they say ABSOLUTELY DON'T. This is because Italians do not observe rules.

In the Piazza San Marco in Porto Rotondo a man says to me: "The more serious money doesn't have to worry about costumes and carats." The more serious money must stay behind locked doors. All I see are costumes and carats. I read in Edith Wharton that in ancient Rome slaves were not allowed to wear distinctive dress "lest they should recognize each other and learn their numbers and their power." No Roman with any claim to social standing would be caught dead in last year's color. And what's true for Rome is true with bells on in Italy's la-la land. This year's color is gold. Gold spandex. Gold lamé. Gold faille. Gold dufflebags. Gold sneakers. I saw a gold Volkswagen bug (and a lemon-yellow Alfa Romeo). Tissue-thin leopard cloth and Cartier summer jewelry: amber with gold, turquoise with gold. I see a girl with gold braces (no one will believe me).

Life is ritualized and acted on the stages of the *piazze* (the Casbah for morning, San Marco for night), the port, the quay. Death to have a Bellini at the wrong bar on the wrong side of the piazza —

one is immediately pegged a barbarian. The *jeunesse platinée*, an improbable number of improbably long-legged beauties, begin to spill out of the San Marco Hotel for breakfast on the terrace at twelve-thirty or so: *Ciao, ciao! Baci, baci!* They are at the port between one-thirty and two; and they are back from the sea between seven and eight; and then they disco. One knows exactly at what hour to find them buying provisions — smoked tuna, smoked swordfish, smoked salmon, peaches and sweet cheeses, white Sardinian wine — for their boats. The few day-trippers who come to the quay to gawk wear high heels; the boat people — who look as if this summer of their lives will never end — wear sneakers.

Lovely hand-hewn granite stones slope to the center of the piazza. Children in designer clothes sell bits and pieces of worn clothes and used toys to other children just like them in the square; grandmothers knit, blond Italian children scoot around on bikes. One might almost believe that the rich are just like everybody else . . . a piazza is egalitarian space.

A little wooden bridge spans a little canal that leads to what is surely the most calculatedly pretty, snug port in the world. The bridge is a copy in miniature of the Ponte Accademia in Venice; Porto Rotondo was planned by two Venetian brothers, said to be the descendants of a Doge. One expects to see Fred and Ginger gliding by on gondolas; one expects to meet, at any corner, someone discreetly insane.

Only little girls wear dresses below their knees. When they begin to have breasts, their dresses rise above their knees . . . why?

I am waiting for a friend in the Piazza San Marco. Uncoupled, I feel invisible. At the same time, I feel that I am the object of derisive speculation. Southern or Nordic, pouty in repose, size two, the girls of summer clothe themselves in skimpy ribbons of expensive material cunningly tied, white,

black, red, gold. A woman in late middle age wears a white spandex bustier, a brown clinging jersey sarong, a king's ransom of gold jewelry; she is ugly and bronzed and she is coupled with an ugly pug. One doesn't notice the men's clothes, the women are the peacocks here. The woman to the right of me is wearing an aqua-and-white T-shirt on which is stenciled a gold lamé King Tut. The stylish Roman shoes I am wearing cost less than the orange juice I am drinking. Just as I am hardening my heart to all pleasure, I see a waiter who, thinking himself unobserved, is having a lively conversation with a fat baby in a carriage; the baby is rolling a lime-green ball between his fat dimpled feet, feet like hands. The waiter kisses his feet, the sun shines.

Saturday dinner at the Spaghetteria, fairy lights and overpriced pasta and willow trees screening out the sights and sounds of the piazza, and uncynical bread. Sunday buffet-brunch at the Aga Khan's Sporting Club hotel, diamonds as big as the medallions of lobster, transparently thin prosciutto hanging from porcelain trees. Champagne with fresh peach juice and fresh strawberry juice, sweet, tingly, candid, fifteen dollars.

Sunday church: I am so used to seeing people in bathing dress that clothes seem to me rather shocking and almost offensive; wearing street clothes on the Costa Smeralda makes people look extremely vulnerable because extremely armored; and I am mildly panicked because when people are not wearing bathing costumes I cannot decipher clues to social class. Here I am, inescapably what I am — the daughter of working-class parents, poor southern Italian immigrants — through the looking-glass.

The church is thrilling. Behind a stern and unremarkable façade is sculpture, by Mario Ceroli, that is the result of a sophisticated mind with an allegiance to the naif, and an inspired hand. The whole interior of the church is one sculpture: layered slices of plywood bonded together to form three-dimensional figures, dense, not static, the interplay of flat silhouettes resulting remarkably in the illusion, tantamount to fact, of roundness and depth: music made solid, the play of life. The church is suffused with the honey-colored light of unpainted wood. The Holy Spirit with a great

THE CHURCH AT
PORTO ROTONDO,
MARIO CEROLI'S SCULPTURES OF
THE LAST JUDGMENT.

*"Then shall the King say unto them on his right
hand, Come, ye blessed of my Father, inherit the
kingdom prepared for you from the foundation of
the world: For I was ahungered, and ye gave me
meat: I was thirsty, and ye gave me drink: I was a
stranger, and ye took me in: Naked, and ye clothed
me: I was sick, and ye visited me: I was in prison,
and ye came unto me. . . . Inasmuch as ye have
done it unto one of the least of these my brethren,
ye have done it unto me."*
— *Matthew 25.*

Costa Smeralda.
Swimming pools.

LISCIA DI VACCA.

unfolding of wings looks toward the oriel window, to olive trees, rocks, the honey-sun: a vision of Jerusalem. Jacob climbs his ladder, Jacob is a stocky Italian peasant; and he is patient endurance and exaltation. Sprays of formal white lilies add their elegance to the surprising elegance of rough wood. On one wall the apostles are gathered for the Last Supper (there is an empty plate: the absence of Judas is his presence); they are listening to the homily, as, in communion, are we. They look across to the opposite wall, to the Last Judgment, where the damned fall, tumbling with arms outstretched, and the blessed rise (they float as if grace were air). They look down at the pews where we sit. The apostles are saints and congregants, and perhaps illustrations of the Abominable Fancy — the discredited doctrine that one of the pleasures of the saved is to view forever (to dine out on) the tortures of the damned. Innocent children, among the saved, play ball. Old men with canes and young men with bell-bottom trousers climb to heaven. Ceroli used the men and children of this town for models fifteen years ago; now the children who rolled their hoops and played ball for him are men and women (damned and saved). At the altar Christ is seen at the moment of ascension; he is lifted and surrounded by women. In this church God has no gender but Christ in this church has genitalia, he is unashamedly man.

Ermanno Spadoni, the proprietor of the Sailing Ship Pub in the Casbah (his place so pink and wicker-white and pretty, candy-striped with sun and shade), tells me, over a peach shake, a *frullato,* that his children posed for Ceroli, they are among the saved. It was Spadoni who called my village "troppa fantasia," but he has thought better of his words; he amends them, perhaps in the consciousness that his mouth should be where his money comes from: "I accept," he proclaims, "humanity in all its diversity — the Colosseum, dolmens . . . your villa . . . man evolves, history judges." What could be more Italian. He winks.

"Animals are easier to cure than these people," says Sebastiana, she is a *pranoterapeuta*, she heals by the laying on of hands. Not so long ago she would have been thought to be a witch. By "these people" she means the very rich, "Japanese with gold dishes and geishas and private police and ships bigger than the Italian navy, and as for the others if it isn't drugs it's AIDS." She does not cure drug addiction or AIDS. She cures benign tumors, conjunctivitis, sciatica, ulcers, gout, pancreatitis, gastritis, cystitis, ailments of the *fegato* (everyone in Italy has an ailment of the *fegato*, the liver, or believes he does or will have), sinusitis, hemorrhage, insomnia, and colitis. That is what she says. She is very popular among people who think transubstantiation and the Trinity are picturesque and quaint (they call her a "simple, lovely person," by which they mean she is not of their class but useful and well mannered, which she is). I like her very much. Sebastiana, forty-four, is like a tree trunk, straight and square in a Upim cotton dress. Her eyes are the color of brownish tap water with light shining through it. Her house looks like that of a prosperous furniture salesman from Grand Rapids. It has the kind of ugliness that only devoted love can create. She loves her thing-y things: her antimacassars, her lamps with shades like petticoats, her framed scenes of rural England, her heavy veneered furniture, her liquor bottles displayed as if they were *objets d'art*. Her garden is rank and gone to seed. A parrot noses the air inquisitively. The Virgin Mary simpers in her garden shrine. A watchdog howls. Sebastiana's ginger cat has ear mites.

Sebastiana's plump hands smell like orange water; they are dry and hot. Where she has placed her hands on my body there are red streaks, welts. The red streaks are hot. I believe in healing hands; my doctor, George Schwartz, had healing hands, though it would horrify him to know that I say so. When he touched me, anguish went away though pain did not. When Sebastiana touches me, I unknot. I have on my lungs the scars left from an undiagnosed childhood tuberculosis — just the sort of thing my mother could be expected not to notice, she was busy with other things. Sometimes I have trouble breathing. (And I am fat.) When Sebastiana touches me I feel relief, the relief is not so much physical as psychic, which comes to the same thing: she tells me I am not dying. I live with the consciousness that I am dying and have since I was seventeen; this is interpreted as hypochondria. When Sebastiana tells me I am not dying, I am immensely reassured: I translate this to mean that although in the long run I am dying, I do not have to feel guilty about it. This brings me welcome relief from my preoccupation with my mortality, and for hours after Sebastiana rests her hands on me — on sheets others have used before me — I sleep.

Sebastiana says she cures by means of beneficial radiation, which gives energy back to the cells that have lost it, and then the cells cure themselves. I have heard stranger things. She believes in that which I do not: the "bloodless" surgery practiced in the Philippines, the presence of the Virgin Mary in Medjugorie. So what. It hardly matters. George Schwartz's religion didn't matter to me, nor did his politics. His kind hands did; her kind hands do. Sebastiana has visions. Once she saw a green serpent with the face of a dog in her garden. She called this beast the Mouth of Hell. She serves Sardinian desserts, sweetened ricotta and lemon curd. One of Sardinia's *abbandonati*, a homeless man, Tommaso, sits on her veranda with the ginger cat and eats Sebastiana's cookies. The ginger cat has pink

liquid oozing from its ear. One morning Sebastiana tells me that for one half hour she stanched the blood of the victim of a car crash outside her door; he was pinned underneath the car, returning from the Mania Disco. She rubs her right thumb against the second and third fingers of her right hand: "Do you have rich American friends?" she asks. From the moment she uses this grubby gesture I think that I will like her less. But I do not. Sebastiana sits in the piazza at night with her handsome husband, Antonio, and eats vast quantities of chocolate *gelato* and whipped cream. She smells very slightly of perspiration.

At the bar in the piazza an Italian Communist says: It is a pity Michelangelo and Leonardo were told what to do by the Church, otherwise we'd know what they were capable of. To which there is no possible reply.

CALIFORNIA FREE THINKING. THINK PINK. FUL-O-PEP. PRINCETOWN COLLEGE. MEXICO LEMON. WHOLLY MACKEREL. These are words on T-shirts. At the San Marco a man is wearing a T-shirt with blood splattered on it and a 3-D rubber hatchet in the area of his heart.

There is a storm. Horizontal lightning, a line of knitting (purl) unraveling. Impenetrable black pierced only by the fragrance of jasmine. We are, this broody morning, on our way to the interior. We drive through boulder-strewn hills, the boulders are tipsy and outspoken, primeval and dignified. They receive light and exude light (blood from stone). Some of the boulders have huge holes in them, as if a capricious giant were having his primal way. This country is wild with the wildness, not of exaltation, prophetic dreams, and hot love, but the dry and thorny wildness of nostalgia, of contained yearning, of memory mingled with desire, love in ashes.

We stop for a wide view at San Pantaleo, where the boats are streaming from Porto Cervo, the hub of the Costa Smeralda, like a flotilla, flags fluttering. I see a woman with fat ankles and slippers wearing what in Brooklyn we would call a housecoat . . . perhaps she is "simple and lovely" (though my companions wrinkle their aristocratic noses), she reminds me of my aunts. A boy wears a T-shirt: *Flatbush*, it says; and my class loyalties flare up like a sore tooth. We stop at the Cala di Volpe Hotel in Porto Cervo, the epitome of international trendiness and managerial hauteur — "a great medieval castle as rendered by MGM for *The Wizard of Oz*." Imagine: it is Venetian and gothic and Mediterranean and Arabian and Indian, with a touch of Gaudí, and English — sweeping lawns down to the water, where punts vie with jet skis, and striped tents like those of Ascot shelter jet-setters who value whiteness above tan. On the terrace Frenchmen and Italians and Englishmen and Americans take tea. We are with someone who proceeds to do a noisy imitation of the Cockney guy, Robin Leach, who does the "Rich and Famous" television show; aggrieved pampered heads turn. Oh, Alice, I say, didn't you learn how to behave when your parents were in the diplomatic corps? I learned to take advantage of every situation, Alice says, hooting at the excess of a place where the gold is more pronounced than the blue of the blue sea. On the terrace, Arabs in Western clothes read Arabic newspapers; days later we hear of the invasion by the Iraquis of Kuwait. In the conservatory of the Cala di Volpe Hotel magnolias nestle in bitter-green leaves. Flights of colored stairs lead to private rooms, Crayola steps, Alice calls them, the manager sends a *portiere* to follow her lest she give greater offense. Of course it is she who is the true aristocrat.

HOTEL CALA DI VOLPE.

Of course people walk down these stairs. But it violates the imagination to think of that; it is impossible to see these stairs or to think of them without being convinced that they wind upward only, candy-colored stepping stones to an intimate fantasy stored in the attic of the mind.

Our somewhat erratic course into the interior and to the west coast of Sardinia is owing to the fears of the judge with whom we are traveling; it is her perfect desire to avoid the bandits who hide in the caves of the Sopramonte mountains.

The Romans tried to get rid of Sardinia's bandits, and so did the dukes of Savoy; they are here still, rustling sheep and cutting off the ear of an occasional hostage held for ransom. The judge's family were prominent industrialists here, she believes the bandits have committed to memory the license plate of her car, in which we drive. Furthermore, she wrote an article for a local paper defending the right of the farmers of Oliena to attack the shepherds of Orgosola, which town she quite reasonably wishes to avoid . . . although her contempt for shepherds is such that she would have us believe not one of them knows how to read. The judge uses the words *shepherds* and *bandits* interchangeably.

When the judge inveighs against shepherds/bandits I want nothing more than to drive into the wild Sopramonte hills.

Shepherds are the poets of Sardinia; they regale celebrants at weddings and feasts with extemporaneous verse.

One of my grandfathers was a shepherd in Calabria; no one seems to hear me when I say this.

The judge says that shepherds are like chameleons; we will never see one with his flock; they hide. I make her a bet that we will see a shepherd, and I lose.

The cicadas crackle like small fires in the high corn. The judge talks of Carthaginian human sacrifices and of Phoenician human sacrifices, and the land — primitive, pagan, barbaric — seems to take its being from her words. Along the road we see bleeding rusty cork trees, skinned of their bark; stones look like altars.

At Santa Cristina there is a deep well, a triangular opening in the ground . . . nobody dares to walk down the perfectly squared steps so neatly laid, so geometrically elegant, so terrifying. Like many primitive places it looks quite modern (Mies van der Rohe). Seven feet away there is a circular opening where blood, it is conjectured, was poured as an offering to the hideous gods. (Blood entered the ground here, or very small infants did.) We peer down and see our faces, disconcertingly placid, in the dark and oily water. Near this place there is a perfectly conical hill surmounted by a twelfth-century castle; the hill looks like a nuclear reactor, though it was made by God. It overlooks nuraghi, truncated cone fortress-dwellings made of stone fifteen hundred years before Christ; next to the Costa Smeralda the nuraghi are Sardinia's most touted tourist attraction, they are perfectly boring, and reduced, in any case, to indecipherable rubble.

Wild white ponies run in these hills. I cannot bring myself to eat in a restaurant called the OK Corral.

The Romans, who could contain neither banditry nor Christianity, exiled Christian soldiers to this harsh land; in this pagan landscape there are many early Christian churches, beguilingly naif, some of basalt, small and black and beautiful and frank.

One day I become angry at the judge because she presumes to usher me away from a small church as she tells me, "This church is not important." *Important to whom?* I want to say, but do not. I feel so bound, in southern Italy, to my absent family. She reminds me of my family, denying my subjectivity, saying *this is important, this is not,* acting as if her choices were necessarily mine. On account of my anger I pray to a golden madonna, whereupon my anger turns to rancid sadness.

We find, in the little town of Mogoro (a center of weaving and folk crafts), a sweet little church in the Pisan style ("not important"); the custodian is a young girl who wears cutoff jeans and eats a peach and reads a comic book leaning against the door of the church, which is surrounded by dried leaves, lending it a nicely pagan, nicely festive air. It is a cave with Corinthian columns and one spectacularizing chandelier; and in the blazing light, from floor to ceiling, wall to wall, are naif ex-votos, framed drawings in crayon and pencil and paint that tell simple stories: splayed figures hug the ground next to overturned ox carts; wine barrels crush construction workers, whose souls rise from their bodies ectoplasmically; a plane shoots crayon fire at a farmer, so Brueghelesque; blood squirts from the chest of a recumbent shepherd trodden by a horse; a woman shrieks in childbirth, her baby has a harelip. In Palermo, antique dealers sell folk art like this for thousands. Here it is on offer to God, along with wax ex-votos of healed body parts and framed clothes — a baby's green velvet dress obscurely stained — and family photographs. (My acquisitive instincts are aroused.)

Baby owls, exhausted from the heat, sit in the afternoon sun on the side of the dusty road.

In the village of San Salvatore there is a church built upon a spring that the ancients worshiped, and a makeshift building with signs in English: Post Office, General Store, Saloon — this is the town where spaghetti Westerns were made. It is supernally quiet here. Rocks grow like wildflowers. Peasants have taken over adobe houses built to accommodate cowboys; old people sit outside with their backs toward the lanes where Clint Eastwood and Italian cowboys staged shootouts; they face the abandoned-looking houses. They face an eternity of time. Their faces are seared, their eyes are full of the future and full of the past—full of a tragic solitude; the present is not easy to locate, here.

There is a taste, in all this dust, of the sea, an exhilarating hint of iodine in the air: a half-hour drive will take us to San Giovanni in Sinis on the sea . . . and, in the violet dusk, to a row of rush houses along the beach . . . like a mirage. (I noticed this when I lived in North Africa: one always seemed to come to an oasis at sunset . . . like a mirage . . . perhaps it is always the oasis that comes to us.) These houses are the quintessential shape of house, the house a child draws — a rectangle topped by a pyramid-shaped overhanging roof. Some of the straw houses have tin roofs; on the roofs are television antennas as well as seagulls, and this is not a mirage. A man waters sunflowers and his straw house. His wife, a toothless crone and friendly, pulls us into the straw house with her liverish and dirty hand. It is impossible, in this space — Frank Lloyd Wright would have loved it . . . or perhaps his vanity would not have permitted him to, it is architecture without architects — it is impossible to tell where the courtyard leaves off and inner space begins; spaces flow together organically. Roosters wander among heavy armless chairs upholstered in cabbage-rose chintz. Chickens flap their wings on tables covered with doilies starched in sugar water. On a blanket in front of the straw house next to this one, Italian hippies with a fine disregard of the historical and the cultural moment are smoking grass. What a cliché, Sheila says of them: the eyes of the camera sees differently from the eye.

The parish church of San Giovanni is the second oldest on the island, it is lovely; in its baptismal font is a raised carved fish — the secret symbol persecuted early Christians used to disclose their identity to one another. It is thrilling to touch the shape, so old, of faith.

The beaches on this peninsula of Sinis are long and white, they shine, they are of white granite age-ground into sand. There is no gold lamé. There are caravans and campers; and in Tharros there are ruins, Arabic, Roman, Carthaginian. It is hard to form affection for an ancient Roman sewage system. The judge says the ruins were splendid once, but the mosaics, like the Elgin marbles, were removed — vandalized — by the British. "You only have to lift a stone to steal mosaics here." My acquisitive instincts are heartily aroused — I want to move a stone and steal the ancient world.

Bruno rises from the emerald waters of Tharros with two small octopi in his hands; we have arranged to meet him here. We have dinner with Bruno and Gianni (they are love-laced, these men, as Italian fathers and sons so often and unself-consciously are) at the home of Gianni's sister, who, recently widowed, says she needs us for comfort; she has only just met us, her hospitality is divine (she makes us feel indispensable), and so is the food: a pasta with *bottarga*, roe from fish found in the Gulf of Oristano; a lasagna with béchamel sauce; a delicate white fish, *dentice*; herbed chicken; roast suckling pork with rosemary; green salad with fresh corn kernels; piquant Sardinian cheeses made of sheep's and cow's milk mixed; bread in the form of sculpture — dough twisted into roses and thorns and birds; and the "popes' wine," vernaccia, the dessert wine of Sardinia.

While we eat with three generations of Gianni's family, we see on the beach a man pushing a white wicker pram and holding a white parasol.

When shepherds are away from their families they carry with them sheets of bread called *carta da musica*, "music paper."

THARROS.

This tower is as friendly as the medieval skyscrapers of San Gimignano.

"I danced in the morning
When the world was begun,
I danced in the moon
And the stars and the sun.
I came down from heaven
And I danced on the earth.
. . . .
Dance, then,
Wherever you may be,
I am the Lord
Of the Dance, said He.
I'll lead you all
Wherever you may be,
I'll lead you all
In the Dance, said he."

— Sidney Carter,
Lord of the Dance

SARDINIAN SHEPHERD.

*Whenever I hear shepherds excoriated in Sardinia,
where they are popularly supposed to be nomadic
bandits, I recall the second chapter of Luke: "And
there were in the same country shepherds abiding
in the field, keeping watch over their flock by night.
And, lo, the angel of the Lord came upon them,
and the glory of the Lord shone round about them;
and they were sore afraid. And the angel said unto
them, Fear not; for behold, I bring you good
tidings of great joy, which shall be to all people.
. . . And this shall be a sign unto you"
(Luke 2: 8–12).*

*My paternal grandfather was a shepherd in
Calabria, and lived a quarter of his life in greater
proximity to animals than to people. He was not
meek; and he was fiercely intelligent. He did
manual work all his life; and he railed against his
fate. He did nothing gently — he died raging and
cursing the final obscenity life had brought him;
but he loved his grandchildren, and was good to
us, tender and kind. He was not meek; but when I
read that the meek will inherit the earth, I think of
my grandfather, once a shepherd; and I think the
mercy of God extends even to those whose meekness
takes the form of sorrowful rage.*

The judge says there is an amazing rate of
incest in shepherds' families, it goes unreported
except when the victim, boy or girl, is beaten in the
bargain; the penalty for this abuse is seven to ten
years in prison. These words stain my mind for days
and inhibit me, I cannot look into any friendly face
without unwarranted questions forming.

Tharros is famous for its bitter honey.

Utopian communities fill me with dread, I think of
the Tower of Babel. On the Costa Smeralda there is
a planned community (one of many) that is so beautiful — green lawns and towering boulders and flat
sheets of rock and houses of the same soft gray
stone, a cedar-decked swimming pool built into a
rock a hundred feet high (a place where fluting gods
should congregate) — I didn't see how it was possible not to love it. I did not love it. I thought it was a
fabulous fake. I think of this place now because we
are driving through a planned community, Arborea,
that Mussolini built in 1928. Earlier in that decade
Mussolini reclaimed swampland — the land of
those redeemed fens still has what Shirley Hazzard
calls the "relapsed stillness of inland water" — and
he irrigated land that once had been only minimally
good enough for shepherds and now is farmland. He
used eucalyptus trees as screens to distance malar-
ial mosquitoes from populated lands; his efforts
were successful — and he is overly praised. Arborea (which has a twin sister called Fertilia) was
settled by men and women from the Veneto; and it
looks like an oddball civics lesson. The broad main
street has Fascist villas painted in Renaissance colors and frosted with *putti* and garlands, quasi–Art
Nouveau; there is a clutch of little thatched huts,
English village-style, with English gardens gone to
seed and picket fences. One expects to see Alfred
Lord Tennyson, notebook in hand (failed romanti-
cism is putrid). There is an extraordinarily ugly

Sheep may safely graze on pasture in a watchful

shepherd's sight.

contemporary Salesian seminary in neo-Bavarian style, and there are workers' row houses that might have come — except for their Mediterranean color washes — from the set of *Grapes of Wrath*. In the window of a deserted Fascist railroad station there is a sign, FANTASY ISLAND, advertising the television show of that name (this is inexplicable, but true). The romantic languors of Fascism were cynicism at its most appalling. Mussolini harnessed Pan; Arborea is a tidy place. . . .

"Fascism wasn't *all* bad," says the judge; I have been expecting these words, hating them in advance.

The woman standing in the courtyard in Gallitea is wearing black and no expression at all. A man emerges from the house and stands next to her in a loving and proprietary way. The years have been hard on the old woman; it is difficult to tell whether the man is her husband or her son. She allows herself to be photographed (so long as her traditional black kerchief, emblem of female submission, is firmly in place) as if being a photographic object were part of the fate to which she is entirely resigned. She is seventy-eight, her vocal cords have been partially severed in an operation, she squawks with perfect dignity and grace. She and the man who is her husband take us through a series of courtyards — like the straw houses of Tharros, these whitewashed houses in a casbah-town are made of spaces that flow in and out — and series of linking stairs. Dusty fig trees stand in the courtyards. Her spotless kitchen of cerulean blue is full of objects that tell us stories and nourish her memories — handsome old baskets with geometrical designs, a hand mirror of ice-blue and opaque white Venetian glass, a telephone partially covered by a tea cozy, a huge TV covered with a needlework cloth. A wall clock ticks away remaining time.

We drink tiny cups of lethally strong black coffee with sticky-sweet amaretto chasers. The kitchen table is covered with shelled almonds; she is making *confetti* for the family celebration of her fiftieth wedding anniversary (five sons, twenty-one grandchildren; seven great-grandchildren). She professes to expect us to come to the feast. Her life has been full of disappointments — she only hopes that we will come and will not think ill of us if we don't. She is without guile. She covers my face with many little moist kisses, which I like.

This old town has a seventeenth-century Spanish organ and is famous for its nightingales.

Fear of shepherds is fear of the untamed, fear of the dark prophetic blood of poets, and fear of impulses we have deemed for ourselves unspeakable.

Shepherds speak to Danilo Dolci:

What are stars? I know what stars are. The sun and the moon make the stars. . . . It must be smoke, all the smoke in the world, that makes the sky. . . . The moon's made out of the sky, the sky's made out of smoke — of the smoke that rises up from the earth below. . . . The stars never stay still — they move about in the sky all night long. When it grows light, they go away; just as the cows go into their stalls, the stars go into theirs. All of us human beings and all the animals, too, are like the stars.

The stars are some queer sort of eyes, maybe — how can I tell what they are? . . . The moon is the Madonna. . . . The sun is Our Savior. . . . I pray to the moon and the sun. When it's cold, I pray to the sun to come out and when the sun comes out and it's too hot, I pray to the sun to go in. "Warm me," I say to the sun when I'm freezing: "give me some light," I say to the moon when it's dark. When

CALTIERI.

"Husbands shared their first human ideas with their wives, beginning with the idea of a divinity of theirs which compelled them to drag their women into their caves; and thus even this vulgar metaphysics began to know the human mind in God. . . . From this most ancient origin of marriage came the custom by which women enter the families and houses of the men they marry. . . . By the Romans, . . . women were regarded as daughters of their husbands and sisters of their children. Thus not merely must marriage have been from the beginning a union with one woman only, . . . but it must also have been a union to last for life."
— *Giambattista Vico*

"Christ, from the moment of his capture, is already
in death. And the dead are dead, as all the
proverbs say, counseling peace, resignation,
omertà. But the mother is alive: sorrowing, closed
in the black mantle of her pain, transfixed,
moaning; image and symbol of all mothers. The
true drama is hers: earthly and of this flesh. Thus
it is not the drama of sacrifice and human
redemption; but that of the pain of being alive, of
our obscure visceral dismay when confronted with
death, of the closed and perennial mourning
of the living."
— Leonardo Sciascia,
"Feste Religiose in Sicilia,"
in La Corda Pazza: Scrittori e Cose della Sicilia,
translated by Mary Taylor Scimeti

the sun comes out and warms me, I'm happy, and when the moon gives me light, I'm happy too. I love to watch the moon moving about in the sky. I pray to the stars as well. "Please shine for me," I say. I love to watch the stars — they're so pretty. . . . We're in the world because we have a house in it and we work in it. We eat in it too. Why do we come into the world? To work. To eat. To work. I don't know anything else. Men grow old. Everything in the world. The animals grow old and so do the Christians. But the sun never grows old.

Blacks from Morocco and Tunisia are called, in Sardinia, *vucumpra*. This is a corruption of *vuole comprare?* — do you wish to buy? They sell trinkets in the squares.

They are not permitted to sell in Porto Cervo.

The International Herald Tribune, Rome (Reuters):

A police crackdown against suspected tax dodgers aboard yachts and cabin cruisers caused hundreds of luxury vessels to set sail in a hurry from Italian ports. . . . A pastry cook at the tiller of a yacht worth 500 million lire ($400,000) said he was authorized by the owner to use the vessel for his bakery business. The owner had declared his annual income as 15 million lire. Other yachts were registered as belonging to nonexistent companies, housewives and traveling salesmen.

GOLD SKIN. EGO. These are the names of boutiques in the main piazza of Porto Cervo. In the window of Valentino there is a white ruffled ermine coat. It is 110 degrees.

From the hoteliers' guide, *In-World*:

The water is all the emerald color you find only in Bulgari brooches and Cartier clips; the pink-powder beaches resemble grated garnets; the air is redolent of the parfum plantations of Grasse; the people seem to have been hired for a film by Antonioni. His Highness's prefabricated lotus land is the most perfectly pretty shore this side of the south seas. What could possibly add to the beauty and perfection? The island is Italian!

Window shopping: a bib of pearls, a harness of diamonds, a scarf of pearls; braided sable, braided mink. Nature denatured in a pink shopping mall. But *frutti di bosco*, fruit of the woods — gooseberries and thick cream. A peach shake with fresh peaches and peach liqueur and *fior di latte* ("flower of milk") ice cream.

In the news shop I see a dusky, deep-eyed Arab beauty from the Cala di Volpe Hotel; she is followed by a vast and subservient Aunt Jemima maid.

The piazza at six-thirty P.M., the sun so soft, and everybody smelling so good. Like a beautiful woman, Italy's piazzas are best at certain times of day; and this one's harmony and radiance are best enjoyed — as is the passing crowd — on a summer day at six. Shadows fall on the white lawn dresses of all the pretty little girls. Who could object to cunningly placed pots of geraniums on medieval balconies, even if the medieval balconies are only twenty-five years old?

PORTO ROTONDO.

Americans never seem to achieve the simultaneity of sexiness and simple elegance that Italian women do. They opt for one or for the other.

A hooker strolls with apparent purposelessness; dressed almost, but not quite, in the manner of everyone else, she has crossed some fine line to declare her obscene intentions. She has hot eyes behind dark glasses. She is offering her buttocks for sale. There are no takers. She sits next to an old lady in black, who engages her in offhand conversation and offers her a Perugina chocolate.

This sign in the *giornalaio* in the square: "English spoken with enormous difficolty." You have made a *sbaglio*, a mistake, I say to the proprietor: d-i-f-f-i-c-u-l-t-y. "If I'd spelled it right, it would be *facile*, easy," he says. He is a heavy-handed teaser, he was born in Brooklyn and escaped with his friends Al Capone, Lucky Luciano, and Frank Sinatra, he says. When he discovers that my people come from Abruzzo he cuts the nonsense out; in spite of his age he leaps over the counter and embraces me; he calls me cousin.

This man looks like my father.

The Sardinian Grazia Deledda won the Nobel Prize for literature in 1926. Her books are not in print. At a restaurant named for her I have the best lunch I have ever had: antipasto of smoked boar, smoked swordfish on music paper with caviar, herbed seafood salad, bitter-orange smoked roe. Then a fat, tubular, chewy pasta made *in casa* with lusciously tender *gamberoni* in a puree of tomato and basil and court bouillon, saffron, and a hint of *peperoncini*.

We sit under a picture of a Spanish grandee with Inquisitorial bones and drink white Sardinian wine and eat a salad of arugula and tomato in an olive oil that is a food in itself. Alice has trout cooked and served in a three-inch casket of coarse salt. I have suckling pork (not on the menu), brought golden brown to the table, its perky ears and wrinkled snout looking surprisingly festive and not at all alarming (so nice of him to die so cheerfully for me), the meat from behind its neck as sweet as meat can be. Ices — orange juice with lemon zest, fresh strawberries and *mirto*, blackberry liqueur. Fresh ricotta and lemon curd for dessert, a *tiramisù* made with chestnuts, and a silky bavarian cream with the slightest touch of peach. Coffee. *Digestivo* — *fichi d'India* (cactus pears), bright orange, syrupy and astringent. A transcendental meal: $240 for two.

Large families dine at neighboring tables; there is everything sanguine and nothing pompous about their approach to food, they are informally dressed, their children are in shorts. We smile at one another, we all act as if we have done something clever, which indeed we have.

In the piazza a middle-aged woman sports a T-shirt with this legend in gold: TOTO, I DON'T THINK WE'RE IN KANSAS ANYMORE.

The feast of Ferrogosto. There are thirty-four dishes at the gala buffet at our Porto Cervo hotel, Le Ginestre; these are some of them: Alaska king crab; whole boiled lobsters; *arancini* — balls of rice stuffed with shredded gizzards and peas and tomato sauce, fried to a golden orange-brown; avocados with shrimp; *vitello tonnato* (veal with a delicate, lemoned purée of tuna); baked eggplant; stuffed zucchini; sole in aspic; poached salmon; roast beef; eggs and brains; roast turkey; *millefoglie* cake; fruit tarts; peaches in wine. Each dish is beautiful, and each is good, and the chefs do not trouble to hide their pride. A singer sings who cannot sing, except when he wails plaintive Sardinian songs, and Brazilian dancers dance who cannot dance, and everybody is happy. The little children running around the lighted pool with its tissue-curtain cascades of purple bougainvillea look like bouquets of flowers, and all the men wear pride of family, and the women in their gauze and gold look like Christmas wrappings and a pregnant woman emphasizes her big belly with a twisted sling of gold-threaded paisley cloth; and she dances.

To the man who wishes Michelangelo and Leonardo had not been constrained by popes, Tell me about the *festa*, I say. I know nothing about religion, he says, and orders champagne. This is the day Mary ascended to heaven.

The tall beach pines give off the soapy smell of resin. The morning breezes carry the soft clean fragrance into my room, and it wakes me. The sun and the moon hang together in a sky smoky with a residue of stars.